CW00501636

Thirty Eight

A tall tale

By Chris Perkes

To Rachel, with love.

Cover design by Rachel Perkes, based on an original design by the London, Midland and Scottish Railway, 1930.

ISBN 978-1-4709-6447-4

A Morning Journey

George regretted having stowed his raincoat deep within the holdall. Each car that passed entrained with it a swirl of foul grey water that seeped deeper into his one good woollen suit. At least the navy cloth wouldn't show it too badly, he brooded.

Shortly the traffic lightened and George darted across the road eliciting a klaxon call from a speeding motorist that had failed to see him. He was within sight of Euston station now and his pace quickened in anticipation of shelter from the rain. A brief check of his cheap watch confirmed his fear that he would be lucky to make the 10:23 to Liverpool. The tardiness of the London, Midland and Scottish railway was all that was likely to get him aboard. He was half running now towards the platforms. Names of alternative destinations flashed by - Tring, Watford, Northampton, Birmingham, Glasgow (would do in a pinch, George mused) but at last he spotted Liverpool.

The ticket inspector looked to be closing his stall but he waved George through as if he'd backed him in the Grand National. Brotherhood of the LMS, perhaps? The doors were being closed one by one, the distant hiss of steam from the dual locomotives set the tempo - this train was leaving very shortly. George dived for the first class coach but felt uncomfortable, he was used to holding only a third class ticket. Aboard he adjusted himself and slung the holdall over his shoulder. His right hand trembled from the absence of its burden. A light condensation settled on his forehead as he walked up the train. A couple of sharp glances from the well to do passengers confirmed he did not belong in first.

The train was unusually empty and George quickly found an empty compartment. He wrestled the holdall into the luggage rack above the seats and removed his woollen jacket. There was every chance this suit was ruined. The jacket was steaming now, drying as it had first on George's back and now on the velour seating. He wiped the beads of sweat from his forehead with his handkerchief. All the hurry and scurry for departure seemed to have subsided. In the distance George heard a single carriage door shut. Several minutes later the door to his own compartment was opened.

"Are these seats taken?" enquired an educated female voice waving a finger at the bench across from George.

"No. No, they are free" enunciated George. The educated voice had subconsciously taken George's voice a couple of rungs up the social ladder.

"Thank you" replied the new arrival.

George brooded briefly. He had hoped to have the compartment to himself, at least as far as Rugby. An hour of carefree sleep would have done wonders for him. George observed the new occupant, as far as was possible without staring. Here was a woman not easy to place in age or social class. Conceivably as old as fifty or as young as her late 30s, George would have guessed her age as early forties, and settled on 42 for no good reason. Well dressed, but not overtly wealthy, her hair was "set" in the way that was presently fashionable. It was obvious she was wearing make-up, but it was subtle. As she took her tweed coat off, George's eyes moved across her curves, down her back, across her bottom, over the slight curve of her belly and lingering over her blouse which concealed who-knows-what layers of complicated under garments.

George quickly adjusted himself in his seat and deliberately cast his mind to more earthly matters, calorific values of common British coals perhaps? The situation in Spain? What a colossal waste of time the past 24 hours had been? Presently the train started moving and George resolved to fall asleep despite the intrusion.

The stops were few enough and efficiently brief. George glimpsed Rugby then Nuneaton. The third stop was Stafford. George awoke in readiness for his own stop which was just 30 minutes after departure. His companion in the compartment was still there and musing over the crossword in the Manchester Guardian.

"I was expecting you to sleep through to Liverpool" she said in a good natured tone.

"I get bored by train journeys and I didn't sleep well last night" he muttered morosely.

"Philipa Arden" she volunteered "and you are?"

"George Bradfield" he replied.

"Pleased to meet you, Mr Bradfield."

"You too, Mrs Arden" he replied.

The conversation duly ended, George had plenty of time to contemplate how he could have answered better before the train heaved off towards Crewe. As it did so they passed an elegant blue train. The engine looked more like an aeroplane than a steam train.

"The Coronation Scot" George explained to himself as much as anyone else.

"Indeed." Did she know this already? Was she humouring him?

"I work for the LMS" he explained, as if in justification

"Well then I can complain to you about the lateness of this train."

"You can but I'm not sure there is much I can do. I'm an engineer, I design the boilers."

"I'm sure you are too modest but I shall keep my comments to myself." She signed off and returned to her crossword. George let his attention shift to the etching of Conwy castle behind her and then to the individual drops of moisture that were the condensation upon the window. Outside it was raining but the sky was brighter than it had been in London. A goods train flashed past with its brine wagons trailing behind it and the logo of Imperial Chemical Industries stamped on everything. Nearly home. As his own train slowed to a snails pace, George remained seated. No need to get up until the train passed the marshalling yards.

They had stopped in countryside, green fields stretched away for several hundred yards on either side. As seasoned rail travellers both occupants of the compartment returned to their reading material. Random stops were not exceptional. Minutes dragged by, no trains passing in either direction. After about half an hour the guard wandered down the corridor and George caught his eye.

"Derailment at Norton Bridge, we're stuck here an hour at least" he stated cheerily in a Black Country accent.

George returned to the compartment and Mrs Arden looked up in the expectation of news. George repeated the information with none of the guard's cheer. Mrs Arden looked to have resolved something within her mind but was assessing all its implications. "I'm going to find the buffet car, would you care to join me for lunch?" Despite otherwise enlightened views George felt uncomfortable being propositioned by any women. Furthermore he harboured a vain hope that they would get moving shortly and he could alight. Reasoning that Mrs Arden was an unlikely seductress and that sharing lunch in an LMS dining car was fairly respectable, his remaining qualms centred on the likely cost of the meal and the presence in his bag of a perfectly serviceable roast chicken and stuffing sandwich courtesy of the Colonnade Hotel. Mrs Arden was already getting up from her seat and gathering her handbag together.

"Why not" conceded George adding together the cost of 3 courses, a bottle of wine and coffee for two. The remaining ten shilling notes in his wallet would probably cover it, and if all else failed he could use the cheque book, this being early enough in the month. With the invitation accepted, Mrs Arden led the way down the corridor towards the likely location of the dining car. George resolved to look out of the windows at the rolling grassland rather than the rear profile of Mrs Arden, with the result that he twice bumped into others heading out of their compartments towards the dining car. When they got there a small, orderly queue was forming.

"Table for two please" Mrs Arden rapped out. A single harassed looking waiter guided them to an empty table. They sat down and were given menus.

"Can I get you a drink before lunch?" enquired the waiter maintaining a calm, aloof air despite further passengers arriving in the dining car.

"A gin and tonic" said Mrs Arden. George was tempted to copy, though a beer suited him better.

"Bottle of Bass, please." The expression on the waiters face wavered for only a second. To drink beer in the dining car is no crime, but contrasted rather sharply with the elegance of Mrs Arden. In any event the drinks arrived with remarkable haste. An oily looking measure of gin rested at the bottom of a heavy glass, tonic separate in a ludicrously small bottle. The bass bottle was opened and an empty glass placed beside it. Both diners poured their drinks. The alcohol and bubbles ignited the conversation.

"There's more choice than I expected" mused George.

"I'm a regular railway diner" confessed Mrs Arden. George was uncertain if it was polite to ask why, finally noting "I've never eaten in the dining car before."

"Really, do you have some inside information?" she teased.

"No, I usually bring sandwiches." I'm making a fool of myself, thought George. The conversation briefly stalled. George observed the waiter. By a miracle of organisation he was seating people, preparing drinks and taking orders to the kitchen. Mr Henry Ford and all the stop-watches in the world could not have created a more efficient process.

"Well Mr Bradfield, I think I'll have the French onion soup, followed by the plaice."

"And I will have the devilled kidneys, followed by the rib of beef."

"May I take your order?" The waiter had suddenly appeared. He had likely overheard the discussion, an impression reinforced by the speed with which he wrote the details down. But although it slowed him down it was clearly an important part of his ritual to formally ask the diners what they wanted. The orders duly given, Mrs Arden was determined to draw George into a full conversation.

Evening Trials

Crewe station was busy with the traffic of rush hour. Every few minutes a plumy but disembodied voice announced "This is Crewe, change here for...." although the swarming mass of commuters seemed to know exactly where they were going. It had been properly dark for at least half an hour, but an artificial daylight was preserved by innumerable lights. Only in corners, under stairways or far up in the glass roof was the natural order left unmolested. In those dark places, George imagined, slept the vampires of middle Europe, waiting for the onset of real night and human sleep before they emerged to feed upon your fears.

George emerged unscathed onto Nantwich road and started walking towards home. It was colder than it had been in London, his breath hung as a light fog in the still air. Supper tonight would be pea and ham soup with dumplings. George's landlady was a certain Mrs Minshull of a very uncertain age and background. She had a compulsion for imposing symmetry upon the world, and within her own house had met with some success. George would regularly find his effects rearranged in a simple but geometric patterns. For reasons unknown even to Mrs Minshull she had long ago settled on a menu of 14 evening dishes from which no man could persuade her to deviate. This particular day of the fortnight had been, and always would be, pea and ham soup night.

The dried peas would have been soaking since the previous night, the salty ham would also have been immersed in water for hours on end. Sometime in the mid-afternoon the two ingredients would have been introduced to each other and sprinkled with a catalyst of thickly chopped carrot. The whole would be allowed to slowly bubble over a low gas flame. By now they would form a rich green liquor flecked by pieces of orange carrot and pink ham. At any moment suet dumplings would join the pot and be allowed to steam for a further half hour. Finally the finished product would be ladled into bowls and served, the shiny white dumplings sitting on top of the ham and surrounded by a boating lake of peas and carrot. His ample lunch had been a few hours ago and George was looking forward to supper.

Upon arriving home George was greeted in the hallway by a very distressed looking Mrs Minshull.

"Mr Bradfield, two policemen have just called for you." George wasn't unduly alarmed.

"What did they want?"

"They wouldn't say exactly, but I heard them say something about un-natural practices." At the phrase "un-natural practices" Mrs Minshull's face contorted in many directions before settling into its more usual position. She adjusted her bosom with her forearm and stood silently waiting for George. George was puzzled. The thought occurred to him that Mrs Minshull was jesting, but the old dear hadn't shown any previous attempts at humour and she was clearly in a state of distress. George was reasonably certain he hadn't committed any crime, so he viewed the visit as nothing more than curious. Mrs Minshull was doing an excellent job of telling half a story.

"Did they leave a card? I'll give them a call from work tomorrow" he asked calmly.

"They didn't leave a card. They demanded that you go to their police station tonight. They were very rude." George had been in the process of taking off his coat, but decided to put it back on. The sooner this was dealt with the better.

"Is it the main police station, in the ______ ?"

"No, they've left an address, it's over by the engine works." George looked at the address and shuddered - it was for the Railway Police. Each of the big railway companies maintained their own police force. It had all started innocently enough - manning level crossings, signals, points, keeping obstacles off the track, preventing vandalism and being the ultimate sanction behind the ticket inspectors cheery "tickets please". However the policemen of the LMS were mostly ex-servicemen and prowled the bigger stations such as Crewe in a martial manner, searching for miscreants. George pitied the traveller who had to "help them with their enquiries". As if this irrational fear were not enough, visiting the Railway Police also meant a walk of thirty minutes. It was not welcome news to George. He took the address from Mrs Minshull whilst ushering her through to her parlour. The occasional table was still out from the afternoon, upon which was arranged a teapot heavily insulted by a tea cosy. George felt the pot, which was still warm. He poured her a cup of tea and reassured her that there was no cause for concern. She was calmer now and he left for the police station.

A half hour walk to work is a fairly pleasant way to start the day. During the evening it can be a nuisance, but at any rate puts some distance between your work and your leisure. To have to do the round trip when other souls are tucking into their supper is unpleasant and George's mood darkened as the journey progressed. He found the building easily enough. It was an unremarkable red brick building from the late Victorian period. Lights shone out from windows on all floors. He entered through the atrium but there wasn't a reception, only a number of divergent corridors. It appeared that a variety of small businesses occupied the different offices. He read the details of some of them: "The Smiling Buddha Silk Company", "Medium Machine Tools".

George looked around and presently, with some relief, he found a small lacquered sign marked simply “Police” directing him along the corridor and up the stairs at the end. The first floor shone with an efficiency of electric light that could only be officialdom. George walked down towards the light. As he neared it he became aware of a room to the right, lit slightly more dimly. It was some kind of waiting room, at least 10 yards deep by 8 yards wide. In the centre was a counter staffed by a policeman in uniform. George smiled and approached him. The policeman, a career constable judging by his age and insignia, looked at George and raised but one eyebrow to indicate George should speak.

“I had a visit from your colleagues” explained George.

“What’s the name, sir?” asked the constable. George replied in perhaps a little too much detail.

"Easy. I've heard all the excuses before, it's not me you have to answer to. Take a seat."

The waiting room appeared to house all human life. Directly opposite there was a poorly dressed eastern European, doubtless caught out by the old “off-peak ticket on a rush hour train” dilemma. If he had only spoken English he might have taken the Guards offer to alight at Crewe, but instead he had stubbornly stood his ground and would now have his moment with the magistrate before tomorrow was through. Next to him there were two boys, scarcely in the teens, their notebooks giving away their shameful secret. Train spotters. They had probably been in a larger group. There’s safety in numbers, unless you're the slowest runner. They too could have escaped, if only they had accepted the clip round the ear. But they were grammar school boys and thought they would back-chat the Railway Policeman. Well they were humbled now, one crying whilst the other implored him to dry up. Further along from these boys was a well dressed gentleman with an immaculate silk tie and a finely tailored suit, and sat next to him a rascally looking youth. It appeared they had been apprehended together. The youth, seemingly known by the police, was proffering occasional advice to the gentleman who was keen now to distance himself from his one-time acquaintance. George didn't care to speculate what state they had been apprehended in.

"He's a bit of a bastard that copper, but he's fair in his own way" remarked a man sat next to George.

"They need to signpost this place better" answered George obtusely, he was certain they were within range of the constable's hearing and he didn't want to brush too closely with the law.

"How long have you been waiting?" enquired George.

"'Bout two hours. You're usually out in about four provided you don't play silly buggers with them" replied the man. George was tempted to ask what constituted playing silly buggers, and indeed from what well of personal experience this observation was drawn, but at that moment the constable looked up and shouted "Silence!" The room was quiet. The only noise was the scratching made by the constable writing at his desk.

"Am I under arrest?" thought George, but for the moment exercised his right to silence. It had been nearly half six when George had first sat down. Slowly the minute hand arced round to the top of the clock face. George was distinctly uncomfortable on the bench. The boy who had been crying had started sniffing back phlegm. The man next to George shifted almost constantly in his seat. George would have taken off his raincoat, but there didn't appear to be anywhere to hang it. No one had been called from the waiting room in all this time and George grew weary calculating how long it might take to clear this up.

There were he, counted, 13 others in this room. Let us suppose that there are four interview rooms (that is the four doors leading off from this waiting room), and that each interview takes 30 minutes (some hope on current form!). There are therefore 3 batches of four to process before me, or 90 minutes plus my own interview, so two hours. I'll be home for about 9, Mrs Minshull will warm up the pea and ham soup and then I can read for an hour before turning in at 11.

Then he took a more pessimistic view. The man had said four hours - that meant it would be more like 11 when he got home, Mrs Minshull would already have gone to sleep. A bag of chips on the way home followed by a very careful creep into bed to avoid waking the old dear's spaniel.

Finally he dragged up the worst possible combination. There was only one room in use, they'd each take an hour, it would be dawn before he was out of here to face either an hours round trip to clean up or turning up for work in yesterdays clothes. His spirits sank.

"George Bradfield." called the constable and George looked up, two younger men in civvies stood by the counter. George walked over and they ushered him into one of the rooms. The benches behind George erupted into a riot of protests.

"One law for them..."

"Oi, where's the justice in that?"

"Bloody fairies" shouted someone.

But the loudest protest came from an enormous woman who had been sat near to George, an unintelligible burst from the heart, the closest approximation George could make was a deep sonorous "Moo". The constable stood up and bellowed "You are not obli.....". The door to the interview room slammed shut separating George from the mob.

It was a room of similar proportions to the waiting room, sharing two of the doors with that previous place. A dim bulb hung from improvised wiring in the high ceiling. The two officers (he assumed they were officers) motioned for George to take a seat at a simple wooden table. Sat down first, George could start the conversation.

"Am I under arrest?"

"No" laughed one of the officers "Not yet anyway."

"How can I help?" Nicely put, thought George, very business like.

The officer smiled and looked down at the notes. He had an opening line of questioning prepared, written on foolscap paper in front of him but decided to abandon that and closed the file.

"We both know why you're here, so there's no point playing silly buggers."

"I'm sorry, but I don't know why I'm here" insisted George.

The officer looked thrown off balance, he looked back at his folder but shrugged and continued anyway.

"Come on Mr Bradfield. George. There's no point making this any harder than it needs to be, is there?"

"I suggest you cooperate" said the other officer.

"I would like to cooperate, but I do not know under what premise you have summoned me here. If you could explain that I will do my best to help you." George was impressed with himself.

"Let's start with your friend Jacob Goldsmith."

"Jacob is a friend of mine from University, we read the same subject" conceded George.

"A good friend?"

"Yes, one of the best."

"A special friend?" At which the officer nudged his colleague who cracked a leery, unpleasant grin.

"I'm not sure what you mean?" replied George, very unhappy at where he perceived this line of questioning to be going.

"Listen Mister Bradfield, we have it on good authority you and this...." He was searching for a word that evaded him.

"Yid?" ventured his colleague, a member of the British Union of Fascists if ever there was one.

"...you and this Jewish gentlemen were discussing un-natural practices until the early hours, at some times with your arms around each other." George felt crushed by the distortion and innuendo that was passing for fact. He was so angry he couldn't summon up anything to say. He felt pressed backward into the chair.

"Further, we have witnesses to the fact that the two of you spent the whole night of 11th January in Mr Goldsmiths third floor flat." For some reason the flat being on the third floor was particularly disgraceful.

"This is nonsense." George had found his voice at last.

"Jacob and I are good friends, that is true. We spent most of Tuesday evening in a Maida Vale pub - it was called The Iron Shard I think - discussing an industrial process Jacob is trying to perfect. We both joked that it appeared to violate the laws of nature - specifically the first law of thermodynamics." The officer had started to glaze over but let George continue.

"Whether it does or does not violate that law we don't know, but we joked as to what the penalty might be for such a transgression." He had lost both the officers by now, but neither would let on.

"Jacob suggested it might be a life sentence of entropy - that is disorder in plain English - a concept he borrowed from the second law of thermodynamics." George was shaking with indignation now but felt like he was running with the wind behind him.

"These are poor jokes, I'll grant you, but they are not a conspiracy to any 'un-natural practice' that the law of England need concern itself with. As for having my arms around him, it was a night of heavy drinking, many people in the pub were singing and putting their arms around each other. There was nothing improper about it. If there was, you need to arrest a pub full of people." George sat back in the chair still trembling but flushed with triumph.

"And I did sleep in Mr Goldsmiths rooms, on a very uncomfortable wooden floor. Mr Goldsmith had the luxury of his bed" he added as an after thought.

"A pack of lies" cried officer number two, officer number one still trying to spell thermodynamics on his foolscap pad.

"No, the truth" insisted George.

Despite his eloquence George was worried. These two were clearly clueless and their allegations were unlikely to stand up in court, but even the hint of such impropriety could embarrass him. People are in the habit of saying "there's no smoke without fire", and a thirty something bachelor often draws enough suspicion without this nonsense. At work the terms 'fairy' and 'pansy' were booted around as general terms of good natured abuse. They had never bothered him because, however successful or otherwise he might have been with the fairer sex, he knew he found women attractive and not men. He thought of Mrs Arden and her curves and how that might in some way be admissible as evidence.

Officer number one had now written 'therm-o-die-namics' into the record but showed considerable flair in spelling 'entropy' correctly. He was obviously pleased with himself and looked back up at George. He opened his mouth as if to speak, but there was a knock at the door and an underling entered with parcels wrapped in newspaper.

"Looks like tea" observed officer number two.

The two officers busied themselves with unwrapping their meals. George looked on forlornly. It was inferior looking stuff, the nearest chip shop was notable only for the size of the vermin resident there. Nonetheless George was hungry.

"Look at the size of this beauty" An enormous savaloy sausage was waved under George's nose. The two officers bantered backwards and forwards in an increasingly lewd and bizarre manner. George remained silent. You are not obliged to say anything. George was left wondering what stroke of ill fortune had led him to this ridiculous situation. After some time the door opened again but this time a more senior officer entered and the behaviour of the two original officers altered immediately. They jumped to attention and started explaining the course of the interview so far. The senior officer had looked harassed from the moment he entered the room. His demeanour deteriorated further as the officers related their tale.

"No doubt about it sir, he's as queer as a nine-bob note" said officer number one.

"Complete puff" pronounced officer number two, as if this was a wise and learned legal judgement.

"You damned fools. I asked you to question the suspect about his business during the past two days. I did not ask you to conduct the Spanish Inquisition" fumed the senior officer. And then, turning to George.

"My name is Inspector Francis Kaye. I would like to apologise for any offence my colleagues have caused, please bear with me." And he turned back to the original pair.

"Get out of my sight, you are a bloody disgrace to the force" he seethed at the two juniors. This ought to have been an end to it, but officer number two wouldn't let go.

"We've got evidence, by his own confession."

"You have nothing, in fact worse than that, you have offended an important witness in a matter of considerable importance. Get out!" And with that the Inspector picked up the savaloy and started hitting the officer around the face. On the second swipe it bent about its centre, after four swipes it burst open, covering the other officer in vile pink sausage meat. George couldn't resist smirking. The hapless duo left the room and the Inspector looked in vain for something to wipe his now greasy hand on. He settled on his own handkerchief and then sat down.

"Once again my apologies, Mr Bradfield. The police force is drawn from all walks of life and we do, unfortunately, have our fair share of imbeciles."

"Don't mention it" replied George, he felt at considerably more ease.

"Let me be clear, those clowns were meant to listen to you, not accuse you of a crime we both know you to be innocent of." George let go a deep breath. The weight of accusation at last lifted from him.

"With that in mind I would very much appreciate asking you a few questions about your business during the past two days. I hope that won't take too long, and at any rate I propose we finish for the evening before 11pm."

"Fair enough" said George.

George explained the nature of his trip to London. He explained how he knew Jacob and how Jacob had got back in touch after many years. He explained the rudiments of the process Jacob had demonstrated, omitting those items Jacob had insisted were to be considered a trade secret. It dawned on George how little Jacob had told him about the process. The Inspector listened and appeared to comprehend, as far as anyone could. He didn't seem unduly interested in the process.

"Out of sheer curiosity would it be possible to explain these laws of thermodynamics to an old plod such as myself?" enquired the Inspector.

"I'll have a go. In very simple terms, the first law says that energy cannot be created or destroyed, just turned from one form into another. So when you burn a lump of coal you're simply turning the chemical energy of the coal into heat and light."

"Makes sense, you can't get something for nothing. And you think this process Goldsmith has discovered will break this law?"

"I don't know. I'm sure it can be explained one way or another. As he has demonstrated it to me it seems to release large amounts of heat and not to exhaust the original source, but that's not the same thing as creating energy out of thin air. It needs an awful lot more research."

"What about the second law you mentioned?"

"That's a bit more specialised, and is mostly to do with heat engines." The Inspector looked puzzled and George was concerned he may not do justice to this explanation.

"Heat engines? Is that the same as a steam engine?" asked the Inspector

"A steam engine is one example of a heat engine, yes."

"I understand, carry on."

"Well the second law states that in any closed system, disorder will increase with time. Scientists give disorder a fancy name called 'entropy', but disorder will do. To take the example of burning a lump of coal, the chemical energy can be considered ordered because it's all in a nice, neat lump. The heat and light given off by burning it float off into the world around us so are more disordered."

"I'm still with you" nodded the Inspector.

"To take your phrase, the first law says you can't get something for nothing, the second law says you can't break even."

"And this process, does it break the second law?"

"No idea" said George, because, if this process broke the first law, all bets were off. And finer minds than George's would be re-writing the text books.

“Is there a third law?"

"Yes, that says the entropy of atoms or molecules at absolute zero is zero."

"Absolute zero?"

"It's the lowest possible temperature, about minus 460 degrees Fahrenheit."

"Chilly. But quite ordered. And not relevant to Mr Goldsmith's baby?" ventured the Inspector with a grin.

"Indeed" replied George. He was enjoying himself.

"Fancy a brew?" asked the Inspector.

"Yes please" replied George.

"One lump or two?"

"Just one."

"Back in a minute" and with that George was left alone in the room. He liked the Inspector. Partly, of course, because of the contrast with the two cretins from earlier, but also because he seemed genuinely interested in the stuff of George's world. Quite why he was so interested George could only guess at, but was content to help.

"There we go." The inspector placed two large mugs of milky tea on the table.

"It's getting on for ten, so I won't keep you too much longer. Can we move on to your journey home. I understand you shared a table at lunch with a lady of recent acquaintance. Would you mind telling me her name?"

"Mrs Philipa Arden." The Inspector wrote this down. George proceeded to relate the details of the journey, the delay, their lunch and subsequent conversation. Finally he mentioned that she stayed on the train as he alighted at Crewe.

"Thank you, did Mrs Arden express a particular interest in any aspect of your work?"

"Not that I recall." George struggled hard to recall the circumstance, but his mind would only recall the curving lines of Mrs Arden as she first removed her coat.

"It would seem she cast quite a spell on you Mr Bradfield" taunted the Inspector. It was a good natured jibe, and George simply smiled.

"Did she mention 'The Blackwatch' at all?"

"The army regiment? No, she did not" replied George.

"Thank you for your time Mr Bradfield, I enjoyed the lesson on thermodynamics. Can I ask one further favour of you?"

"Of course" George replied by reflex.

"Should you have cause to meet Mrs Arden again please get in touch with me." And at this the Inspector handed George a business card. It gave only his name and a number in London, no other details.

"Is she under suspicion of something?" George asked feigning naivety.

"A lady matching Mrs Arden's description has appeared rather too often in my current investigations. I am interested in meeting her myself. I am prevented by my office from saying anymore."

"I will tell you, should I see her again" reassured George. In reality he didn't know whether he would or would not tell the Inspector, but reasoned he was unlikely to be put in such a dilemma.

"Thank you Mr Bradfield. Please consider this matter closed. Once again my apologies for your treatment at the hands of the two imbeciles earlier. Would you like me to show you out?"

"That won't be necessary."

"Good night them, Mr Bradfield."

"Good night."

And with that George walked out of the interview room, back into the waiting room. The counter was closed up, the light switched off and the room empty. George wondered how the others in the queue had been dealt with so quickly. Out in the corridor he retraced his steps and descended the stairs. The small businesses were all closed now and only the lights at the atrium illuminated his way. Looking at his wristwatch he read it was just past 11 o'clock. His mind was full of questions, but his brush with the law had woken his senses to the outside world. He heard a lone bird up in a leafless tree warbling, even though the dawn was still at least eight hours away. He took some comfort that all the iron, and coal and red brick of the LMS couldn't snuff out this intrepid bird song. Every pub he passed was shut up and unlit, every chip shop closed. There was no food to be had in Crewe after eleven.

He wandered past the empty railway station on his way home, still illuminated, but vacant. His pace quickened back to Mrs Minshull's.

The Boilermaker

The engine works was the main employer in the town. If anybody asked where you worked, you only had to say "The Works" and people knew. George was employed as a mechanical engineer and considered himself a professional as surely as a lawyer or doctor would. Sadly the outside world did not see being an engineer in quite the same light and this led to many a misunderstanding. Mrs Minshull had not been too delighted at the prospect of a boiler-suited grease monkey as her potential lodger. It had taken a letter of recommendation from Mr Stanier's office to put her right. Mr Stanier enjoyed the title of "Chief Mechanical Engineer" for the LMS. Talented though George was, it was unlikely he would ever carry such a grand title. He was too fond of solving the minutiae of engineering problems. It was this preference that had led him to the seaming cul-de-sac of designing the boilers for Mr Stanier's new locomotives.

When George had joined the LMS it was 1932. It had taken him 6 months to find a job since coming down from University. His exasperated parents had supported this enormous hatchling for much too long and the daily friction between Mrs Bradfield and her son was still fresh in their memories. The opportunity of leaving the country vicarage for the town had seemed a breath of fresh air, at least metaphorically.

George showed flair for solving engineering problems and had enjoyed promotion twice. He had recently observed that whatever promotion or reorganisation came his way, he was always two rungs below Mr Stanier. This he found amusing rather than irritating. He admired Mr Stanier for the way he had united the disparate tribes of the LMS. In the late twenties and early thirties there had been little short of all out war between the "Midland Railway" and "London and North Western Railway" which had been united under the banner of the LMS back in '24. These days they pulled as one. Though not, perhaps, as profitably as the shareholders might have wished.

George shared an office with a Mathematician called Stickland. There could be no doubt Stickland was a gentleman. His immaculate suits and Home Counties accent had jarred when he first arrived at the LMS. But Stickland was also remarkably disarming. He could join in with the canteen ribaldry and tell the filthiest jokes as surely as anyone. His enormous frame tending now, in early middle age, towards fatness contrasted with George's more modest build. Numerous rumours orbited around the person of Stickland. Where he came from and where he currently lived were unknowns to everyone. He had a talent for being present at (though apparently not involved in) any kind of mischief be it a brawl or industrial action. The most persistent rumour was that he had been a seaman, and specifically a junior rating at the time of the Invergordon Mutiny. It was said that he had been one of the principal agitators against the cuts in Navy wages. Stickland was an enigma. He did, however, make excellent tea.

George took in a mouthful of his tea and opened his notebook. After rudimentary pleasantries, Stickland had returned to his quadrille paper. George reviewed what he had written down in London. It was measured and professional, but seemed nonetheless rather improbable. Like any large company, the LMS received the occasional approach from garden shed amateurs who claimed to have created the frictionless bearing or built a perpetual motion machine. Wherever real life departed from some theoretical optimum they dreamt up elaborate schemes to engineer away the difference. Some were fraudulent but others were sincere men of some learning who had become seduced by a species of fools gold. To avoid such traps, George had had an earnest little talk with Mr Stanier prior to his trip and drafted a short list of tests that this process would need to fulfil. Somewhat surprisingly it had met all of them. As George mulled over how to draft this into a memo for his manager's attention, Stanier appeared in the office. Both George and Stickland greeted him heartily. Stickland returned to work almost immediately, whilst George discussed the London visit with Mr Stanier. The boss indulged George, listened to his explanations, and took some time to arrive at a decision. It was agreed George was to present the new technology to a board meeting in March.

In the following days George became increasingly ambivalent at the prospect of presenting to the board. In his early years with the LMS he had harboured heady ambitions to climb the corporate ladder. Still infused with the optimism of the 'twenties, he imagined himself as a senior executive, in an oak panelled office overlooking the city of London, dictating his firm but enlightened views to the receptive workforce across the Empire. Age and experience had tempered his enthusiasm. His limited experiences of managing others had led him to conclude he was better off with a steam table and a slide rule. But an invitation to address the board was a novelty and George allowed his old ambitions to be rekindled. Stickland, who had overheard the conversation, expressed the view that if only George was bold enough to carry a revolver he could deliver a very welcome return for the employees and shareholders of the LMS with only a modest loss of life. For the sake of sanity George clung to the assumption Stickland was joking. The mathematician resumed typing.

George also had ambivalent feelings about the LMS. It had given him a job at a time when he was starting to fear he might be unemployable. It had nurtured him, after a fashion, allowing him a degree of prosperity. He thought of the trappings of that wealth. Hardly a king's ransom, but he had his savings and his current account, both status symbols in themselves. He had plans too for buying a house, a peculiar kind of nesting instinct motivated by the concept of being master in his own home, not at the bidding of mother or landlady. Yet, he had to acknowledge, he hoped to meet a girl and share his home with her, which would in essence repeat the cycle. Unconsciously he drew a doodle of a reciprocating steam engine expelling cooled, wet steam only to take a fresh draught of hot, dry gas. These predictable analogies amused him even though they posed the unanswerable question of where the locomotive effort was taking him.

George took another draw on his tea and rubbed his eyes. The London, Midland and Scottish Railway, what company to keep! The largest joint stock company in the world, or so they claimed, though if you had money to invest you'd get much the same return, and rather less risk, from treasury gilts. It was principally a marriage of convenience between the Midland and the London and North Western Railways. The Midland, for its part, had brought with it a dubious dowry. It had operated a fleet of splendid little engines which performed well on the modest curves and gradients between London and Birmingham. Short, frequent services were popular with the marketing department and the customer alike. Where extra power was needed, such as the climb out of Euston, they simply tacked another engine on the front. The problems had arisen when they were used on the old London and North Western routes, particularly the winding, hilly tracks north of Manchester. Here the small locomotives had proven to be a liability. As the accidents and derailments caused by underpowered trains mounted the LMS had reluctantly reversed this "Small Engine" policy and hired Mr Stanier to design a new generation of bigger locos.

The latest wheeze animating the LMS was the quest for speed. They had got themselves locked into something of an arms race, vying for world records with other railway companies at home and abroad. Each was trying to notch up the newspaper headlines that their marketing department craved. It was an uneasy alliance between the marketeers and the engineers, but both had proven equal to the task. George had played his own small part in squeezing the most steam from the boilers of the biggest engines to date, the Princess-Coronation class. In tune with the spirit of 1937 the first engine had been called Coronation, the next two Queen Elizabeth and Queen Mary, but with only so many contemporary queens to choose from subsequent ones were named after royal princesses and then duchesses. Finally by the sixteenth engine they had resorted to "City of Birmingham" and George had heard it rumoured that they would end up with one called "City of Stoke-on-Trent", which prompted Stickland to quip they weren't so much scraping the bottom of the barrel as examining the residue at the bottom of the Royal Doulton.

George's thoughts returned to the meeting in March. There were numerous problems with any proposal. In the first instance was the abject lack of any theoretical basis for the process Jacob had demonstrated. Both George and Jacob had speculated on what it could be. It wasn't a normal chemical reaction because the chemical composition was unchanged. Some substances do give off heat when dissolved in water – Enthalpy of Hydration was the scientific name – but whilst this could account for an initial vigour it wouldn't be as sustained as the phenomena Jacob demonstrated.

A further problem was the secrecy that Jacob had insisted on. George was permitted to discuss it within the LMS, but not to any other bodies. Jacob was insistent that any fundamental research into the background of the process was to be done by his own company. He had not shared any significant details with George, only the ability of the process to raise heat and therefore steam.

Which led to the final problem. Raising steam is easy enough. You or I can do this with a pot of water on top of a stove or a campfire. It is a fine way of making a cup of tea and is good employment for an expectant father. Hero of Alexandria, Thomas Newcomen and James Watt all refined this (raising steam, not children). But the 200 ton railway trains of the LMS required steam heated to temperatures well above the boiling point and compressed to tremendous pressures. It remained unclear as to whether Jacob's process was equal to this task.

The more he considered the proposal the less enthusiastic he was about delivering it. He didn't fear humiliation at the board meeting, he feared stoking up irrational expectations amongst senior management that wouldn't know any better. He sought Stanier's help but the boss had disappeared, apparently to fight another ill-informed initiative, his last words apparently being "bloody streamlining".

Another Morning

The day of the board meeting George was woken up at 5:00. He had slept fitfully, waking every hour or so and glancing at the phosphorescent hands on his alarm clock. He was filled with a general discomfort about the prospect of his presentation and a specific concern that he might miss his train. He planned to be on the 6:30 train to Birmingham. That would get him into Birmingham a little more than an hour later, some time before 8. The meeting was at 9, so George had factored in a safety margin of a full hour. Even the LMS would struggle to delay him by that much. And if he should be delayed it wasn't his fault but that of the LMS – essentially those he was going to meet. George was rather pleased with the circularity of this argument, but he earnestly hoped it would not be necessary.

Arriving at the station just after 6, George joined the early commuters. The newspaper stands were opening and George bought a paper. Most shades of opinion were reflected, although rather unequally. One paper for the Communists, one for the Fascists, two for the Labour Movement, two for the Liberals and more than half a dozen Tory titles. Not being a frequent newspaper buyer George opted for the Manchester Guardian out of regional, rather than political, sympathies.

The air was cold and clean, a rain shower having swept the air overnight and the traffic of the day not having got into its stride yet to pollute it. On the horizon the first inkling of a dawn was showing. George contemplated buying a cup of tea for warmth, but felt the newspaper had been enough of an indulgence, and worried also about its medium term effects. It would be unfortunate if his first words to Sir Josiah Stamp were to ask where the little boys room was. Instead he took comfort in the warmth of his overcoat, which at a little distance he fancied looked rather smart. Buoyed by this thought he surveyed the platform for any attractive women. But it was a dismal crowd of suited, middle aged men who waiting for the 6:33. His eyes searched upwards, sweeping across the roof. Not keen to pick out one of the resident vampire bats, he fixed instead on the top of the stairs. People were arriving in a steady stream, descending down to the platform to wait for the same train as George. It was a steep flight of stairs and most people looked down at their feet during their descent rather than meeting the eye of anyone on the platform.

So it was that he spotted Mrs Philipa Arden some time before she spotted him. She descended with a certain glamour absent from those around her, and elicited the occasional lecherous stare from some of the less discrete men. She stopped and stood a good twenty yards away from George, nearer to the platform edge and in apparent expectation of the train door stopping very near to herself. George took the opportunity to survey her unobserved. Her full figure was evident and even more alluring than he remembered it. She was dressed conservatively but rather elegantly. George was uncertain whether he should say hello. He remembered his promise to the Inspector and wondered again if he would keep it. She lifted her wrist to read her watch and then turned to her left to find the station clock and looked at George directly with cold disengaged eyes. And then she smiled a broad and unforced smile. She was genuinely pleased to see him! George walked over towards her, as she did towards him.

"Mr Bradfield" she exclaimed.

"Good morning, Mrs Arden, how are you?"

"All the better for seeing a familiar face. Train journey's can be terribly dull alone. How far are your going?" A moment of mirth for both parties went by without remark. George answered instead:

"To Birmingham."

"Me too! On business?"

"Yes, I'm presenting to the board."

"Shall I make the predictable enquiries as to the extent of their boredom?" Mrs Arden teased. George started to bluster, but broke into a good natured laugh. It was, he reflected, rather queer how much more informal they were being now compared to their previous meeting. They exchanged pleasantries for the remaining time until their train arrived. The carriage drew to a halt with a door at the exact spot Mrs Arden had previously been occupying. Throngs of people filed forwards to the door and then collectively realised that there were passengers wanting to get off and backed away slightly. George and Mrs Arden were towards the back of the queue.

"Do you have a reservation?" asked Mrs Arden.

"No, how about you?" replied George.

"No. At least I can ask a Gentleman to give up his seat for me." She smiled. George had no answer. They boarded the train and joined the queue down the corridor. All the carriages were full.

"Do you fancy some breakfast – my treat?" George was rather shocked.

"Oh I couldn't possibly let you pay for me." I'm not certain I could afford to pay for both of us though, he thought silently.

"Well I forgot to get a newspaper, so I will buy you breakfast if you let me do the Guardian crossword."

"It's a deal" both of them pleased with the face saving formula. The dining car was busy but there was a table free for them. A short lean man with a lilting Irish accent took their order. George would have been happy with a slice of toast and a cup of tea but Mrs Arden ordered the full breakfast for both of them. Presently half a grapefruit was presented to each diner.

"So you're speaking to the big cheeses today?"

"Yes, I'm making some proposals regarding the process I saw in London."

"Have you met the board before?"

"Some of them, when they've toured the works."

"But never like this before? Are you nervous?"

"Just a bit. I've been practicing all week. My landlady has been kind enough to listen."

"Well every condemned man deserves a hearty breakfast!" And with that she sunk her spoon into the grapefruit.

"What takes you to Birmingham? If you don't mind me asking?" enquired George.

"I'm meeting my patron. Discussing progress on my latest research project." Mrs Arden seemed in two minds about how much to reveal. George didn't like to pry but thought of Inspector Kaye and decided to continue.

"What areas are you researching?"

"I'm looking into folklore, with a particular emphasis on the 18th and 19th centuries." Mrs Arden was unhappy with her answer, though it satisfied George.

"Will this be the subject of another book?" he probed

"It rather depends on the wishes of my patron. I think it would make an interesting book." George now sensed she was not happy on this line of questioning. Lacking the skills of Inspector Kaye he returned to eating his grapefruit. The sweet, acid flesh made his unfed stomach rumble. The arrival of hot food sometime later was very welcome and he tucked into that with enthusiasm. Bacon, sausage, black pudding, fried eggs, fried bread and boiled mushrooms. These, thought George, are a few of my favourite things.

"I think the refreshment car has excelled itself again" pronounced Mrs Arden

"Just the ticket!" declared George between mouthfuls. But he was wrestling with his conscience. Should he tell Mrs Arden about the police interview. If so what should he say? He mulled over the facts. Inspector Kaye had asked that George tell him about any further meeting with Mrs Arden. But he hadn't imposed any vow of secrecy upon him. But if he said anything could he be said to have "tipped her off"? Might that spoil the police investigation? An upbringing of middle class guilt played through his mind. And then he remembered his moral compass. What would my father do? Freed from being henpecked by his wife or harassed by his parishioners what would he do? He would tell the truth. He would explain the situation, perhaps a little pedantically, but without varnish or supposition. So George did just that. And Mrs Arden listened. She seemed at first alarmed, but presently became rather amused.

"It sounds like I should talk with Inspector Kaye. If you have his details."

"Oh course" and George pulled out his wallet and passed over the business card.

"And you should tell him candidly about our meeting today."

"Right." Why did telling the truth feel like a conspiracy in itself? The toast arrived as the train pulled into Wolverhampton. Minutes later, as they departed George looked out of the window and down at the other station, Wolverhampton Low Level. The sun caught a mighty engine in the green and gold of the Great Western Railway. It wore the dirt of a workhorse and it was impossible to tell at this distance whether it was a Castle or a King, but it stirred George to the purpose of the day. Two rounds of toast later, a final cup of tea and they were in Birmingham.

The LMS Hive

George and Mrs Arden alighted into the perpetual twilight of Birmingham New Street. A grand latticework of iron and glass arched overhead. On completion it had, allegedly, been the largest glass roof in the world, but fifty years of utility had robbed it of any splendour and on most days it was arguable whether it provided any more illumination than the gas lamps that burnt night and day. There hung in the air an evil smell, distinct from the familiar soot-and-steam of the railway.

Mrs Arden drew George to one side, out of the tide of humanity and close to a pillar which provided a back water from the flow.

"I think you need a few running repairs before facing the enemy" and with that she withdrew her handkerchief and wiped a remnant of breakfast from the corner of his mouth. She then straightened his tie and stood back to view him.

"I *do* like a man in a smart suit" she said. "Now, Mr Bradfield, I must be off. What time train are you hoping to return on?"

"I'm not sure, probably one around six."

"There's one at ten to six. I'll meet you just here at twenty to. Thank you, Mr Bradfield, for accompanying me this morning, it has been a splendid way to start to the day." She smiled and reached up to kiss him on the cheek. In receipt simultaneously of orders, complements and maybe even a degree of affection George struggled for words.

"Thank you." he smiled "Oh, and please accept this" he handed her his copy of the Guardian.

"Good luck Mr Bradfield." And she disappeared into the stream of people. George had about 45 minutes before he was due at the office. He wandered across the Queens Drive towards the old Midland Railway platforms and destinations south. The structure was almost a mirror image of the one he just left, with Queens Drive as a kind of no-mans land, or uneasy armistice line, between the two former enemies. There sat the same trains with two little engines at the front, but pointing towards London rather than Liverpool. George found himself humming a verse oft repeated in Crewe:

M is for Midland with engines galore
Two on each train, and asking for more

Having found little of interest in this other place he walked directly to the LMS offices. He was admitted by the stentorian door man with a nod that said "I have my eye on you, sunshine, don't try any funny business." He feared he might have been mistaken as some kind of unsolicited salesman. He announced himself rather uncertainly to the receptionist and gave Stanier as his contact. This disarmed her considerably and after a phone call to Mr Stanier's office which confirmed George Bradfield was indeed expected he was instructed to go straight to the board room. The directions were tortuous and George felt certain he would be unable to recall them. He also felt that at any moment he might be pronounced to be an impostor and flung on to the street. But once past reception he was accepted by the other worker-drones as one of the hive. He imagined himself making his way to its heart, or perhaps creeping asymptotically across the paper of Stickland's domain towards coordinates (0,0).

The board room door was ajar and loud confident voices could be heard within. George walked into the room, observed by the other occupants but ignored. They judged him, correctly, to be an underling, perhaps running messages from one seat of power to another. George was uncertain what to do and looked around the room with some discomfort. Should he approach these people? Most of them were stood up recalling their weekend activities. Only the chairman, Sir Josiah Stamp, sat. He finished what he was doing and looked up.

"You must be Mr Bradfield" he said with a cheery voice.

"Yes, Sir" replied George. He felt like he was fawning by using the "sir" but he was equally uncertain how one addressed a baronet. Mr so-and-so or Lord this-and-that were easy but the minor aristocracy put him in a pickle. He was fairly certain the correct address was "Sir Josiah", but this seemed such a cumbersome construction he shrank from using it.

"Have you come down from Crewe this morning?"

"Yes. On the 6:33. Punctual and the breakfast was delicious" George chirped

"Good chap. I'm particularly proud of our refreshment cars. Would you care for a cup of tea?" And he rose and walked over to a table with a bone china teapot sat on it.

"Milk? Sugar?" George picked up a cup and saucer. They were so delicate the cup rattled against the saucer in his hands. The addition of milk and tea steadied matters, but George fretted that this rattle might make him seem less credible in the company of the chairman.

Fortunately the pleasantries continued until Stanier and others arrived. Stamp brought the meeting to a start. George was rather disappointed to learn it was not a full board meeting. He had been looking forward to hearing of the wider LMS world – the hotels in every town, the crumbling canals or the steam packets that criss-crossed the waters to Ireland and the continent. Instead it seemed the meeting had been convened specifically to consider Jacob's process. Now that the meeting had started he took his lead from Stanier, sitting attentively, looking engaged but without speaking. He wanted to get the measure of the meeting, the forms of speech and the language that was appropriate, but it was not to be.

"Perhaps Mr Bradfield could start with an overview of this process." And George was thrust into the bear pit. He breathed in, looked down at his notes and then in the direction of those present.

He delivered his brief well. He gave a faithful and professional description of what Jacob had demonstrated. He answered questions with courtesy and drew parallels with that which the audience could be expected to understand. After fifteen minutes he was beginning to enjoy the limelight, Stanier looked pleased with George as he drew to the end of his oration. There was a brief pause. Stamp allowed a slight smile. Stanier judged rightly that he was expected to contribute.

"Mr Bradfield has given a first class exposition of the technology. If it would please the meeting I would like to draw attention to some of the implications about its potential use."

"By all means, Mr Stanier."

Stanier went through the list. He started with the rather marginal contribution expected of diesel and electric engines. This was not new for the board but they listened in patience. He then expounded on reducing the reliance on coal (this pleased the meeting) but also the reaction this might meet with firemen, miners and mine owners. On the continued need for water of George's proposal, but the potential use of the existing water towers and troughs. On the potential power of the new technology, for faster engines (Stamp and the board members liked this) but also the constraints which the LMS had to live with:

"Truth be told what limits us today are the minutiae – other rail traffic, signalling, breaking distances, as much as the abilities to raise steam. If we were to introduce to traffic such an engine, the competition would copy us fairly quickly and those that are blessed with fewer cities to stop at and straighter lines between them will get to Scotland quicker."

Stanier stopped, he had been tempted to throw in a disparaging remark about streamlining, but better judgement prevailed. He stroked his bushy moustache instead. The board were contemplative. A couple of them spoke, asking simple questions, some through no good reason than to hear their own voice and to be seen to be contributing. There were suggestions to use the research facilities of friends or acquaintances at Birmingham or Manchester Universities, but the Goldsmith's determination to hold onto the fundamentals for themselves would limit such an evaluation. And finally one spoke who silenced all others, the vice-president of railway operations, an engineer himself, though now a shrewd lieutenant for Stamp. He exhibited the supreme confidence of one with long years on the board. He gave an even handed appreciation of George's presentation. He agreed with Mr Stanier. He relied on nothing but sweet reason and then came the devastating finale.

"But, Gentlemen, we are a company that operates railways. Our enterprise is the carriage of people and freight. We have no business researching this curiosity."

Silence. A typewriter could be heard in the room next door. It reached the end of the line, and there was the sound of the platen being moved back to the right. It was like the fall of the hanging judge's gavel. The matter had been decided.

Return and Revelation

Stanier took George out for lunch as consolation. The Chief had been rather impressed by George's performance before the board and wanted to discuss some proposed improvements in preparation for an attempt on the speed record. Not being familiar with the local restaurants they settled on an impressive looking place not far from the LMS offices. If the façade outside was first class, the reception was scarcely fit for freight. Despite the place being almost empty they were shunted icily to one of the least agreeable tables. The chef, in rebellion perhaps at the mediocrity of the place, was however generous beyond belief and they were treated in turns to enormous portions of consommé, mackerel and rack of lamb. Defeated, finally, by a bread and butter pudding of unfeasible dimensions, they discussed the events of the morning. Inwardly George felt a certain amount of relief that the board hadn't gone for it. He had at least avoided promising the impossible. And yet they both still had an intense curiosity in the process. George expressed concern that he might have harmed Stanier's reputation.

"I left the Great Western to join the LMS because Stamp wanted me to be innovative. If my star should fall for every mad idea I've put before him, I would have settled back to Swindon some time ago. They indulge me such flights of fancy because I design such good engines in my spare time." A small smile, a pause, and the slightest flush of embarrassment, and then he added "With an awful lot of help from my team of trusty Engineers..."

"In any case it wasn't such a mad idea. Do you suppose we were the only company your friend approached? I can imagine the boardroom of the LNER or Parsons or maybe even ICI mulling over the proposal. One of them may have a different perspective to ourselves. In engineering there is something to be said for being second and learning from the other chap's mistakes."

Back at the office George ran over the calculations for the improvements discussed at lunch. It felt good to get back to work on real engines. He took a cup of tea at three but had to decline a current bun, lunch having cast a long shadow over the afternoon. He eventually left the office at twenty to six, hurrying for his appointment with Mrs Arden. She was waiting where they had arranged and fixed him with a stare as he came over the bridge. It was almost Six. He tried to look apologetic. She looked furious, but melted rather quickly and couldn't help but smile by the time he stood in front of her.

"Only the tardiness of the London, Midland and Scottish Railway has saved you tonight, Mr Bradfield. They appear to have mislaid our engines."

"How careless."

"Indeed, but let's discuss it aboard the 17:50 rather than the 18:34" and with that they strode towards the train. It wasn't as busy as the morning train and they quickly found a compartment occupied only by an old dowager dressed in Victorian morning. The train leapt into motion some minutes later, the dowager quickly lulled to sleep by the rhythmic motion.

They updated each other on the passage of their respective day. Mrs Arden had apparently received warm praise and encouragement in her research from her patron. She showed no particular enthusiasm for discussing it in any more detail than she had that morning. The conversation therefore became rather asynchronous, George recounting his meeting, emphasising Stanier's trust and the kind words of Stamp. Given this was a path that the LMS were not taking George felt freer about discussing it, and he had a receptive audience. Nonetheless the conversation had begun to ebb by the time they reached Wolverhampton. After some minutes Mrs Arden looked at her newspaper.

"What do you make of Herr Hitler's latest adventures?"

"Austria?" asked George. The news had been filled with dark mutterings about the Austrian situation for some days, then on Saturday Germany had invaded, or crossed the border to restore order, or something. George had only vaguely followed the reports.

"I'm not sure what all the fuss is about. As far as I can understand the Austrians were fascist already. They all speak German. What business is it of ours?" It was a genuine question and Mrs Arden seemed to be taking her time to reply.

"It is true that you could argue, as the chap in the newspaper is doing, that it's no different to the union between Scotland and England. But I can't view it as anything but bad news. They might as well rip up the Versailles Treaty if they let him get away with this" replied Mrs A.

"Versailles! What could we do anyway?" asked George "Full frontal attack across the Rhine, Russians helping in the east? Italians to the south. I think my Dad had enough of all that in the Great War. And I can't see Comrade Stalin and Signor Mussolini helping out anyway. I wouldn't even put money on Blum and the French giving us a hand."

"You're a wonderful optimist, Mr Bradfield" chided Mrs Arden.

"I'm just a realist. My Dad saw enough of his pals blown to kingdom-come between '14 and '18. I can't get excited about the prospect of going to war. If I'm just left alone I'll make a pleasant enough life for myself and my family. Another few years and I might be able to get a mortgage on a new semi. Maybe get a car. Hopefully meet a girl, marry, have some kids." George looked at Mrs Arden to see what effect mentioning other women had on her. He didn't appear to have lit any fires of jealousy.

"Such ambition!" She replied, with a hint of bitterness in her voice and an odd look in her eye.

"It'll do for me. Better than being conscripted" shrugged George and went back to his newspaper. But then it dawned on George what had upset Mrs Arden.

"You lost someone in the Great War didn't you?" A pause and the train clattered noisily across some points. Another train passed in the opposite direction.

"Yes I did." She replied forlornly "Second Lieutenant Alfred Arden, Officer, Gentleman and beloved Husband. Bloody fool as it turned out, too. Went and get shot in November 1918." She stopped talking. George looked at her. In any normal circumstances he might have worried that she would burst into tears, but what worried him now was quite how measured Mrs Arden was in her grief.

"It was a long time ago. It was a different age. I have made a pleasant enough life for *myself* in the past few decades. University, travel, writing, friends of all four genders." She smiled. George tried not to look shocked. "If Alfred had only had your sense he'd probably be here." She paused and turned the newspaper page. But Austria was on the next page too.

"You can sneer at Versailles if you like." She carried on "But what worries me is that all that hard work to make sure we never have another Great War is coming unravelled. And there are nasty pieces of work, like Herr Hitler and Comrade Stalin, with their eye on the main chance ready to make the worst of any conflict."

"We've got our own nasty pieces of work too" added George, thinking of Moseley and the imbecile policeman of some weeks previous. "All I want is the Royal Navy to guard the coastlines and let me get on with fixing the boilers on the Night Mail." He returned to reading his paper. Mrs Arden had flicked past the Austria stories and found something else of interest.

"The Russians have executed Bukharin" she remarked.

"Name rings a bell. What did he do?" queried George.

"Well I'd struggle to tell you without this article. He was one of the last of the original bolshies. Wanted to give more power to the peasants, fell out with Stalin. Quite a good caricaturist though."

"Was he pals with the other one they knocked off recently, Zinoviev? Of letter fame?"

"I'm impressed, yes he was." Mrs Arden was indeed surprised at George's knowledge.

"I was an armchair socialist at University, I knew my Trotskys from my Kerenskys."

Mrs Arden was quiet for a moment. She was coming to a conclusion.

"You mentioned "The Blackwatch" earlier. I know exactly what the Detective Inspector was referring to, though he's got the name a little confused. It is more accurately called The Night Watch. Would you like to meet them?"

Philipa and the Statesman.

George alighted at Crewe, whilst Mrs Arden remained aboard. Her destination was two stops distant. They waved at each other through the window as George started his climb up the stairs. Philipa Arden returned to reading the paper, but her heart wasn't in it and before long she was staring out of the window at the black landscape beyond. Now she reflected fully upon her day and she recalled her conversation with the Statesman.

Few politicians are awarded the title of statesman with anything other than a sense of irony. The British have even enshrined in their national anthem a certain contempt for the political classes with the line "Confound their knavish tricks" hidden in the rarely used second verse. But "Statesman" was a title that Philipa's patron had acceded to many years ago.

He had risen to prominence in the Liberal revival of 1906 and was widely seen to be the enlightened power behind Premier Campbell-Bannerman. He held a cabinet post that had an extravagant, deeply historic, but irrelevant title. His real duties had been to deliver the mass enfranchisement that had been legislated into existence in the past century, and to push further on into universal male, and maybe even female, suffrage.

As the life of the first prime minister drew to a close there were those in the party that tipped him for the succession but he was a personal friend of Asquith and had no stomach for the unseemly jostling that would have been necessary to have snatched the crown. Newspapers of the time commented on a rather Christ-like self-denial, but he enjoyed enormous goodwill in the country at large. He was tipped, by those who are prone to such talk, as the natural successor to Mr Asquith, in the fullest expectation that this would be more than a decade distant. In the meantime, he lived life to its fullest. He married a Welsh lady possessed of modest beauty and from an even more modest background, which further endeared him to a nation tired of being ruled by aristocrats. As the clamour for war built he was increasingly referred to in the definite article. The Statesman.

Shortly before Christmas 1913 his wife was delivered of child. The midwife strove valiantly deploying all the skills of her education and experience. The physician who was summoned after some hours exhibited a similar prowess. But they were constrained by the age they lived in, there was then nothing that medical science could do when faced with such a loss of blood. A pale and serene new mother finally slipped from their grasp after 8 hours. The Statesman was left a father and a widower.

There are examples of contemporary politicians who have taken such events in their stride. To lose a wife in child birth was certainly unfortunate, but was by no means unusual. Nannies and Governesses existed to care for the motherless progeny, whilst step-mothers (not all of them fairy-tale-wicked) were common too. But our man was no ordinary politician, he was a statesman, and he couldn't countenance such an abdication. He resigned his cabinet post (although not his parliamentary seat) and assumed a higher office as parent to the infant Myfanwy. In so doing he became a serious contender for that inglorious accolade "The Best Prime Minister We Never Had". By the time his daughter was attending day school his party had descended into a bitter civil war and was fast retreating from any hope of ever holding office again. Myfanwy, on the other hand, had become a child of singular charm and source of considerable pride to her father. He built himself a new career as a constituency MP and minor patron of the humanities and it was in this capacity that he had come to know Philipa Arden.

Philipa thought back to their conversation of this morning. She had been late, having been wrongly advised to alight at a station called "Somerset Road" close to the university. She had been rather alarmed as her train sailed through the abandoned station and had then had to walk a considerable distance to her meeting. Arriving flushed and rather cold her patron greeted her cordially and asked for two large mugs of coffee to be brought to his office. He took her coat and she was pleased as his gaze remained on her face and didn't stray, like most men, to her ample curves.

They discussed Philipa's research. She felt like she was a first year history undergraduate again, fumbling around whilst her tutor looked on with a wry smile, knowing she would run into the truth eventually. He encouraged her, but was determined not to just give her the answer. Her brief had been to trace the history of an organisation that her patron believed to be called The Night Watchmen. Her research to date had unearthed plenty of material, though much of it folklore and legend, which performed a kind of parallax back to the renaissance whereupon evidence became, predictably enough, a good deal thinner. The main problem in her research was that the name itself was apt to change. Philipa had documents that referred variously to "The Night Watchmen", "The Night Watch", "The Black Watch" and her personal favourite (if only for its grammatical impossibility) "The Night Watchman". The task now was how to fashion this into a coherent work that gave at least some insight into their reason for being. After several hours they broke off for lunch and their discussion became more general. For some forgotten reason the world situation had come up and Philipa had felt inclined to ask the Statesman's view.

"Well, of course, the classical liberal approach is to defend the coastlines and the trade lanes and let people get on with their lives" he had ventured. With her mouth full of sandwich Philipa nodded with interest and he continued.

"Not so long ago that meant the western approaches into the Irish sea, the North Sea and the Channel. And of course the coast of the low countries and France." A pause whilst he sipped his orange juice. "Lord knows that was tricky enough. Even with a navy that, after Trafalgar, nobody dared to engage. For all the bombast that was spoken about after the Great War, the real reason we fought was the prospect of the Belgium coast being occupied by a hostile power."

Philipa had finished her sandwich and was about to ask a question, but the Statesman continued, and she hung like an eager undergrad upon his every word.

"But now we are blessed, or cursed depending on your viewpoint, with an Empire that covers a quarter of the world. And not a nice tidy quarter, all in one place, but hundreds of territories distributed in the most economically interesting parts. Our coastlines and trade routes now include Gibraltar, Malta, Egypt and the Suez canal, The Red Sea and The Persian Gulf, The Indian Ocean, The South China Sea, The Malacca Straights and the Southern Ocean. And even that fails to mention the Americas, which we can do little but pray are administered fairly by our prodigal son, the United States."

He looked gloomily out of the window. "If we could only ensure a further twenty years of peace. Put the empire on a more equitable footing. Revive our national prosperity. If we could turn India from a quasi-colony to a true dominion and develop a colour-blind policy in Africa, well then I would have some hope. But if we have to go to war in the next decade…" His speech was drowned out by a fast monoplane with pretty oval wings flying nearby. When it had passed he continued. "Oh we could put up a hellishly good fight, I don't doubt. But we would have to get used to being Little England again, not the British Empire."

As the train slowed for her stop Philipa brooded on the purpose of her own loss some twenty years previous. But it was a futile question that in any case she had long ago answered. Across the carriage the old dowager was waking up from her many decades of sleep.

The Alchemists of Maida Vale

Samuel Goldsmith was proprietor of his very own chemical company. This had been useful when Jacob graduated with George back in '32, since the young Goldsmith hadn't been any more successful than George in finding employment. Goldsmith Chemicals Ltd. had been founded on the back of Samuel's experience at larger concerns. He had seen how a large company had struggled to find a use for the by-products of its day-to-day processes. Impure hydrochloric acid, useless ethylene and a host of other chemicals were sold as junk or even given away. There was money to be made for the company that was lean and nimble enough to do something with them. On this basis Samuel bought an old industrial building in South London, close to Wimbledon common. The sign outside the site now proclaimed "Goldsmith Chemicals Ltd". After some debate Jacob had managed to persuade his uncle not to add the motto "Making good use of the things that we find".

Despite the reduced circumstances of the early thirties the enterprise had proved successful, and Goldsmith senior had purchased a fine town house in Maida Vale, which was large enough to house Uncle and Nephew without either knowing too much about the other's life.

Jacob displayed a flair for the practical, able to purify the most bilious of substances into something that could be sold at a profit. He had always had an interest in chemistry (or the science of pops, bangs, colours and smells as he saw it). Chlorine in particular had fascinated him for its wonderful reactivity. After a choking fit brought on by a runaway experiment, and to instil some sense into him, his Uncle laboured the point regarding its use at Ypres and Loos and since them Jacob took greater precautions to protect himself.

The events leading to the discovery of "The Goldsmith process" hadn't started in Wimbledon but rather further down the Thames. Samuel had been given a shipment of ore which the original owner had discarded for reasons Samuel didn't need to know. Documentation showed it had come originally from Johannesburg. There were hints that it contained traces of precious metals. It was offered free of charge if it could be offloaded in the next 48 hours and allow the vessel to return to Durban. Since it was free Samuel was willing to take the risk it was nothing more than iron or nickel. Its high density suggested it might at any rate bear metal. Jacob was delighted at the prospect of extracting gold. He spent some hours in the British library researching extraction techniques. The most promising involved cyanide, which Goldsmith Chemicals did not possess in their current inventory and Samuel was unwilling to procure until a detailed assay had been done on the shipment. There was the briefest of debates as Samuel was preparing to leave for a visit to old friends.

Jacob was left in charge of the company and resolved to investigate the ore. His first step was to grind it into a fine powder, and then to see what portion of it would dissolve in acid. It is not unusual for this stage to evolve heat. Neither is it unusual for some of the ore not to dissolve. Jacob retired to give the liquor time to cool and for the indissoluble portion to settle to the bottom. He reasoned that this residue may have the highest concentration of any precious metal such as gold.

On returning to the liquor a full day later Jacob found that it was boiling. And it appeared to get more vigorous over time. Jacob was alarmed. The tank in which this sat was lead, a metal with a low melting point! Jacob deliberately calmed himself. The reaction was taking place in water - the temperature couldn't exceed the boiling point of that water. Nonetheless he would prefer not to have to explain a large boiling tank of water to his Uncle. He decanted various portions of the liquor off into any available container.

Jacob discovered that the reaction would die out rather quickly when the reactants were put into smaller containers, as if the sheer quantity in the original tank had initiated and sustained the reactions. To confirm this he spent a rather long afternoon pumping the liquor into four smaller tanks and watching the reaction ebb away and then pumping all back into a larger vessel and observing the temperature rise again. By this means he arrived at what he dubbed a critical volume, below which the reaction wouldn't proceed. He had also eliminated the solid material that sat as a sludge in the bottom of the original tank. Whether this contained any precious metals was now a distant thought, but he was now certain it played no part in the more interesting phenomena.

Jacob took a break as the daylight began to fail. Over a cup of Earl Grey and a Tunnock's caramel wafer he wrote down all he had observed into his foolscap notebook. He then noted down his proposed next steps. Number one, he would get an assay done on the remaining solid material. Number two, he would get an assay done on the active solution he had been moving around this afternoon. Number three, he would take a further assay of the solution in 2 days time, when the original reactants would be diminished and the products of the reaction might be expected to have built up. And finally, step four, he would repeat the whole experiment from first principles. He looked at the notebook with some satisfaction. What had started as an alchemical quest for precious metals had transmuted into a serious scientific investigation. He signed and dated the notebook. Jacob Goldsmith, Chief Chemist, Goldsmith Chemicals Ltd., December 19th 1937.

Calling the Inspector

George knew that he would call the Inspector, even before having been encouraged to do so by Mrs Arden. The troubling prospect was the invitation. If it had just been an invitation to meet some political loonies George would have had no trouble resisting. It was true he had been an ardent socialist in his youth. Indeed back at University he would debate solemnly with anybody who would care to listen, and some who did not. But he had rather got that out of his system by his mid-twenties, and as the years passed he became less and less enthusiastic for seizing the means of production, distribution and exchange. He retained a certain modernity of outlook and held fairly liberal views on most issues, but the idea of meeting some secret society was not attractive. Mrs Arden had instead invited him to meet his counterparts in the London and North Eastern Railway, who had been investigating a curious phenomenon discovered by a certain Jacob Goldsmith. The fact that these same engineers also figured in Mrs Arden's social research for her patron was one of those arch-coincidences that make one suspect either a higher plan or a gross conspiracy, depending on your level of faith. George retained an open mind.

He decided against calling the Inspector from one of the works 'phones because he feared being overheard, so he left ten minutes before lunchtime, with a look of warm approval from Stickland, and called from one of the public boxes on the main road. He fretted that he might not have enough coins, but a rummage through his pockets turned up a mountain of low denomination change. He pulled back the heavy door and entered the kiosk. A damp metallic smell filled his nose, but the apparatus itself looked immaculate in shiny black Bakelite. He dialled the number the Inspector had given him, was answered after just two rings by a haughty female voice and he duly pressed button A. The coins were heard to drop and he gave his name and asked for Inspector Kaye. He was put through with admirable efficiency. How different to that vile night back in January!

"Hello Mr Bradfield."

"Good morning."

"What can I do for you?"

"When we last spoke you asked me to tell you should I see Mrs Philipa Arden again."

"Indeed I did. And have you?"

"I saw her at Crewe station yesterday morning."

"Splendid. And have your learnt anymore about the mysterious Mrs Arden?" George inserted another tuppence. He took a draft of the damp air and retold his story. Some minutes later the Inspector asked if George would be in London anytime soon. George replied in the negative but the Inspector seemed satisfied nonetheless. George had yet to mention Mrs Arden's closing invitation.

"Well thank you Mr Bradfield, you have been very helpful. If you should meet this lady again, or indeed learn anymore about her, please do get in touch." George now felt he was concealing something from the Inspector, but the window for a confession was closing rapidly. Some change in tone or timbre suggested the Inspector knew he was withholding something.

"If that is all I'll bid you good afternoon, Mr Bradfield."

"Good afternoon, Inspector Kaye."

That needn't be the end, for he could yet call the Inspector again, apologise and mention the invitation, but a queue had formed outside the telephone box. George felt compelled, now he had replaced the receiver, to allow others to use the phone. He opened the door and started to walk slowly back to the engine works.

"What would my Father do?" he whispered to himself.

When George was a young boy his Father had taken him into the city. He had in mind taking George to the museum and both would no doubt have enjoyed themselves. But when their train pulled into the terminus something spooked the youngster and George became convinced they wouldn't make their train home. The child implored the father to stay on the station. You might know the station, but even if you don't you can easily imagine the sort of place. It was nothing remarkable, just a large Victorian railway station covered with an arched iron-and-glass canopy. There were a few shops and a cafe, but it was a place to pass through, not to journey to. Nonetheless, George felt comfortable and they spent an enjoyable afternoon on the platforms, noting down the numbers of the engines that went to and fro and taking tea and cake in the buffet. And then they went home. To this day George doesn't know what his Father thought of that trip, but it seemed to George that such an outing defined his Father's gentle, tolerant, manly world. To make the best of any given situation. It's an ideal George has striven to emulate throughout his life. Did accepting Mrs Arden's invitation, and keeping it secret from the Inspector, further this goal?

Another memory or, more precisely, a series of half-remembered scenes. Their occasional travels into the city brought them into passing contact with the drunk, the destitute and the dirt-poor. What was his Father's attitude? It was complicated. On the one hand he would give the occasional coin, but on the other he was keen to protect George from harm. As the years passed such encounters became a means to re-enforce the parental message. They drove home the importance of "succeeding" in life. But George also sensed an encouragement, not ambition by proxy exactly, rather the gentlest of pushes. It was an invitation to try to peel just a little bit of the primordial squalor from this still imperfect society. The message, never to be spoken: To you, my only son, two injunctions - to make all that you can of yourself and then (and only then) to make all that you can of the world.

The Refugees

You spotted them on the platform some time ago and despite trying not to stare, your eyes are drawn back to them every few minutes. They're certainly dressed respectably enough. In complexion they're no different to any other inhabitant of this town. You're too far away to hear their voices, so it can't be language or even accent. And yet something has alerted your sense to them. They are a foreign body and the psychological immune system that is your mind has been provoked into a response. Perhaps it is the four-in-hand knot in the fathers tie or a certain slant of the mothers hat. Perhaps it is a look in the face of the children, who despite being implored to by their parents cannot help but stare at the bewildering country they have escaped to, with its curious inhabitants.

You would sooner not reflect too much upon their motives. For if you were them you know you would try to escape. Your imagination will not listen to the more staid parts of your mind. It will not stop at taking in the here-and-now. It starts from the premise that they are probably German Jews (German! As in measles!). And that they are probably waiting for a train to one of the Jewish enclaves in the industrial cities – maybe Manchester or Liverpool. But it doesn't stop there either, because you've read the newspapers and seen the newsreels. You've heard of them (it's always "them", the undefined mass) being thrown out of their jobs and their homes, made to do menial jobs, to clean the pavements with toothbrushes whilst neighbours of long standing laugh and jeer. You have heard of other humiliations, which may or may not be true. And you ought to care, but part of you fears them. It fears the unknown implications of allowing this tiny fraction of a desperate people sanctuary in *your* islands.

England isn't the only destination, of course. It isn't even the main one. The climate, the currency, the culture and even the cuisine are deeply unattractive to most people. And simple geography dictates that it is far easier to escape into the Netherlands or Denmark. At this very moment, as you ponder the family on the platform, still others are seeking to flee. Even in these desperate times it is no more than a trickle. Passports have already been confiscated or rendered void by the extinction of the Austrian state. Visas have been denied. They might be an *untermenschen* but they are *unsere untermenshcen* and they cannot be permitted to just melt away. One of them is Lise, an academic of late middle age, who makes a one-way journey into the northern hinterland of Holland. A contemporary of Heisenberg (who should have struggled more with his uncertainty principles) and a close colleague of Hahn, she has waited to the last possible moment. In her mind is the moral ambivalence: that she fled only when her own position became untenable. Should she have spoken out when even weaker specimens were picked off? Should she have stood firm and fought to the bitter end? And how bitter might the end have been? Futile questions, for she is waved across the Dutch border by a complicit immigration officer, just another day-tripper to the historic city of Groningen.

And what then? She has escaped the familiar for the unfamiliar. She is viewed with some suspicion by those about her. She seeks help from distant friends or some-time acquaintances, who grant it for now, but wonder themselves what burdens they may have to shoulder in the longer term. Can work be secured? And, if it can, is it as rewarding as the Kaiser Wilhelm Institute or merely a hand-to-mouth existence. The future is open-ended. Much has yet to be resolved but for today we have reached a place of some safety.

Back in Crewe, their train is late but it doesn't matter. They are grateful for the sanctuary of a land where the trains don't run on time. Father has relented at the children's clamour for a chocolate bar from the machine on the wall. He struggles to find the right change amongst these strange chunky coins. His tired fingers wrestle with the ludicrously smooth handle of the vending machine. Whatever the rights and wrongs, you walk over and proffer the correct amount to a smile that is grateful for any random act of kindness. The children bite into the Cadbury's chocolate, so different to the varieties of their homeland. A moment of uncertainty, both the texture and the taste are different. Then a warm smile. We might be happy here, Vati.

Repeating the Experiment

Without a lab, or even a position, Lise occupies herself reading the various peer-reviewed journals that communicate the breakthroughs in her subject. This has become a necessary task in these changing times. Back when she was a trailblazing student in Imperial Vienna the atom lived up to its Greek name, indivisible, inviolate. But it was becoming increasingly at odds with the world the physicist observed. Mr Thomson had a go at explaining it with his plum puddings only to be trumped by his pupil Mr Rutherford, with his neat little solar-system of electrons and a nucleus. This had made it into the sort of sixth form education Jacob and George received in the 'twenties. The nucleus, the very essence of the element, was the new fortress, yet to be stormed. But Lise knows a good deal more than Jacob and George and is striving to put a framework of sound theory around the practical work of her erstwhile colleague, Otto Hahn. Were a comparison ever to be made, one might be struck by the similarities to the process our friends from Wimbledon common have stumbled upon.

In the early weeks of 'thirty-eight Jacob duly repeated the experiment that was to become "The Goldsmith process". The limited equipment available in the Wimbledon premises meant he had to first ditch the existing batch. It was drained through one-inch piping where whatever processes were going on ceased and the temperature dropped. It was then, in line with the practice (if not the best practice) of the day, discharged into the River Thames. Somewhere around Wandsworth Bridge it reached infinite dilution and ceased to pose a significant risk to health.

Using the same ore as previously Jacob followed the same steps and duly produced a large tank of boiling water. Again. Samuel Goldsmith was also in attendance and was impressed not only by his nephew's scientific rigour but by the rigorous use of personal protective equipment. He knew the younger Goldsmith had suffered very severe diarrhoea and vomiting over the Christmas period and surmised he had poisoned himself with previous experimentation.

With Jacob now restored to rude good health, Samuel was glad to see the lesson had been learnt.

At the prompting of Samuel very discrete contacts were made with industry. Samuel knew he couldn't develop this process much further with the resources of his own company. He considered putting in a patent application, but the very act of such an application makes information public and he was concerned that he wouldn't be able to frame the patent tightly enough to secure a return. He was reluctant to garner any involvement from the state. He had a healthy distrust for officialdom (there had been a minor misunderstanding concerning personal and corporation tax back in 'thirty-three and a regrettable episode involving trinitrotoluene in 'thirty-six). Furthermore he held a specific inkling that they might just swallow the research to date and bar any further development under the guise of "official secrets". In the end Samuel approached two railway companies – George's LMS and their east coast rival the London and North Eastern Railway. He also approached the Imperial Chemical Industries and Vickers-Armstrong. He had wanted to approach C.A. Parsons, but had no personal contact there. Interest was cautious but encouraging. The parties concerned were asked not to disclose any specific information, but old man Goldsmith was careful that very little of substance was shared with them. He knew that human nature would prevail eventually and was prepared for approaches from other companies. Amongst these was a middle-ranking imbecile from Deutsche Reichsbahn-Gesellschaft who made routine enquiries but, upon realising that Goldsmith Chemicals Limited was actually run by people whose surname was Goldsmith, interest predictably waned. Samuel shuddered at the prospect of Jacob and himself presenting to that boardroom.

Samuel allowed himself to contemplate a more comfortable retirement, not to say a certain degree of immortality with an industrial process named after himself.

She rang him at work. How she had come by the number George didn't want to speculate. No real preamble, scarcely a "How do you do?" and he was duly asked out to dinner. George was so flabbergasted that he accepted without argument, merely grabbing a pencil and jotting down the details. It was only once he put the receiver down that he started to have regrets.

In the first instance there was the problem of Inspector Kaye. George knew he really ought to tell the Inspector but some misplaced loyalty suggested he should keep quiet. He was satisfied for the moment, but knew that the unease would only get worse with time. His second problem was that it was well into the month and he had very little money left. He certainly didn't have enough to take a lady out to dinner at what sounded like one of the better restaurants in Chester. This he could resolve by raiding his savings account, although it felt like a sordid action and unworthy of him. Then he remembered how he had felt as he approached her on New Street station. How might it be if she were really his girl? Seize the day, George.

He could have assembled further barriers to attending, but he abandoned each in turn. The more he thought about it the more he wanted to have dinner with Mrs Arden and damn the consequences. Instead he went about planning his journey there. He'd use the train, naturally. The Holyhead express would get him into Chester in less than thirty minutes, and the trains ran late enough into the night for the return. He reviewed the address. He knew Chester reasonably well and was confident he could find the restaurant. As the day wore on he was increasingly excited at the prospect of meeting the mysterious Mrs Arden again.

It was still light when the train pulled into Chester General. April was past now and one could sense the warm days of May were approaching. George walked briskly into the city centre. It was a long walk, but he welcomed the chance to gather his thoughts. It was curious how different it felt coming into the city for an evening meal. As a young boy he would sometimes be brought in by his father, to shop for a particular present or to see a special event. It wasn't a place you casually visited for dinner. And yet, that was exactly what people seemed to be doing. Moneyed people, it should be noted. He passed a number of restaurants where he could see them chatting happily, the soft lighting illuming their carefree faces, the waiters fawning at their boorish requests. George fancied that another couple of hundred yards of this might turn him back into a red-in-tooth-and-claw socialist, but he was spared such a transformation because he located the restaurant in which he was to meet Mrs Arden. It was up in the rows, invisible from the street and only found by George because he had been given the street number. He ascended the steps and regarded the sign over the door. In gothic script there was nothing but the numbers 1848. George opened the front door and stepped into the restaurant. The door sprang closed of its own accord and he took in his surroundings. The place was like nothing he had ever seen. It couldn't be further removed from the exquisite blandness of the affluent eateries he had passed just five minutes earlier. The entire far wall was occupied by a mural of a skyline dominated by what looked to be two Cathedrals. "Speyer" it announced, which George presumed must be the city it depicted. The place was packed with every artefact possible, all alluding to various events in German history. Mounted on the wall was a banknote for fifty million marks, from the days of runaway inflation in the 'twenties. Further along, and in a position of some prominence, was a portrait photograph of Dr Gustav Streseman, Chancellor of Germany when Hitler could barely start a rumpus in a beer hall. The restaurant had a wonderful, conspiratorial air to it. George would not have been surprised to find Engels treating Marx to a Weiner Schnitzel or Euler scrawling on the wall, conjuring with the relationship between e, i and pi. It seemed to celebrate the whole glorious chaos of a nation. It was the antithesis of the clean, efficient, sterile image of Nazi propaganda. The restaurant was small and cluttered, there were about a dozen tables, mostly unoccupied. Only two tables were taken, one by a self-absorbed foursome and the other by a dangerous-looking femme fatale smoking from a black cigarette holder. George dared not catch her gaze and looked instead for a member of staff.

"Good evening Mr Bradfield, I've been expecting you" purred the woman at the table. George reluctantly looked at her. Mrs Arden. She was dressed in a style that must have gone out of fashion at least ten years previously. Her bare arms had an air of delicious indecency to them.

"Good lord!" replied an otherwise dumbstruck George "Good evening, Mrs Arden"

"Do you like my outfit?"

"It's very...striking."

"I look like a tart, don't I?"

"Was that the effect you were aiming for?" asked George with mock naivety, a smirk on his face. He wouldn't want to take her home to meet his parents like this, but that left plenty of other options.

"I was aiming for "Weimar Flapper"."

"I think you have succeeded. You are decadence personified."

"Would you care for an aperitif?" George hesitated for a moment. He wasn't in the habit of ordering aperitifs. He'd have preferred a beer. A glass of Pilsner, perhaps, in honour of the occasion. Mrs Arden took the lead however. "Werner, would you get Mr Bradfield an aperitif?"

"Naturally" replied the now visible host, returning quickly with a cocktail glass.

"Welcome to our restaurant Mr Bradfield. I am Werner" and he shook Georges hand vigorously with his own fat hand. "Koenigsberg Vodka and Fig. Speciality" and he gestured that they should drink. The vodka hit George's empty stomach and seemed to produce an instant inebriation. Mrs Arden drank from her glass with similar results

"We need some food" concluded Mrs Arden.

"Have you been waiting long?" asked George.

"You mean how much have I drunk? I'm just one aperitif ahead of you." That was exactly what George had meant, but he wished he had been more discrete.

"Special menu, Liebchen?" asked Werner, hovering by their table.

"Danke schone" answered Philipa.

"Bitte schone" replied a retreating Werner. George was perplexed by these minor formalities. He looked once more at Mrs Arden, who was herself looking down at the ashtray, stubbing out her cigarette. His gaze wandered back to the décor. Everywhere the eye fell brought fresh treasures. A photograph of the Black Forest sat next to an advertisement for dark beer. An oil painting of Immanuel Kant sat next to a newspaper clipping showing Dr Fritz Haber collecting his

Nobel Prize in 1918. Above them both was the score for "Ride of the Valkyries". Beside all this a large railway poster advertised some minor Pomeranian branch line, the engine throwing out dirty grey smoke (from the brown coal that fuelled it, George thought to himself).

"This place is incredible."

"Isn't it just? Werner and Dietrich have worked wonders."

"Dietrich?"

"The co-owner, you will probably meet him later".

The starter arrived. It was liver dumpling soup. Fortunately the soup tasted considerably better than it sounded and was welcomed by the pair of them, both rather light headed from the aperitif. They spent a happy few minutes in further discussion of the ephemera littering the restaurant. Mrs Arden was, it transpired, one of the regulars at 1848. George was glad to hear no mention of the Night Watch, only tantalising glimpses into the everyday life of Philipa Arden. George told her of his latest conversation with the Inspector, but she didn't seem very interested and the conversation moved onto the need for wine. Philipa motioned to Werner.

"Could Dietrich recommend a suitable wine?"

"Also" and he disappeared into the Kitchen. Seconds later Dietrich appeared. He was an unremarkable gentleman in physical appearance – medium height, medium build, early middle age. The only thing about him of any note was that he was dressed from head to toe in mid blue cotton, cut in the style of a nuns outfit. George stared open mouthed for several seconds before resuming a less confrontational stance.

"Philipa, a pleasure to see you" Dietrich effervesced.

"And you too Dietrich" They kissed extravagantly on each cheek.

"Dietrich, may I introduce a new friend, Mr George Bradfield." The Blue Nun took Georges hand as if it were that of a debutante and kissed it softly.

"Pleased to meet you" answered George stiffly but with restraint, uncertain now where reality stopped and his over active imagination began. What exactly was in that Koenigsberg Vodka? Dietrich was now chatting happily with Philipa. He was discussing his life with Werner in the same terms ones Mother might use to describe ones Father. Intimate, yes, but also homely and ever so slightly banal. George finished the last of the liver dumpling, hoping it might absorb some of the alcohol. The conversation drew to a close and Dietrich departed to fetch a bottle of wine.

"Are they? You know?" George wanted to be more specific, and rather less shocked, but felt he lacked both the vocabulary and the life experience.

"A couple? Lovers? Oh yes" replied Philipa.

"Do they behave like that in the street?" George didn't want to be unduly prudish, but the words just kept coming to him.

"Dietrich's outfit is just part of an act. By day they are two handsomely turned out German gentlemen. No doubt they would like to be more open about their relationship, but they've learnt to be discrete outside of these four walls." George sat silently mulling this. He guessed that a homosexual in England could expect to be bullied and harassed by the Police and the Courts, and might even end up in gaol for a year or two. He could only wonder what they might have to experience in Germany.

The wine arrived, a rare German red which Philipa pronounced to be fine and which they both enjoyed. The main course was a slow-cooked pork shank on a bed of mash accompanied with red cabbage and stewed apple. Raised on thin slices of anaemic roast pork and boiled potatoes, this was a revelation and without a doubt the finest pork George had tasted. The first bottle of wine was soon empty, drained before the main course was finished. Dietrich duly fetched a second bottle. Philipa and George were by this stage exchanging stories that got successively taller and more ribald. Werner took the empty plates away with a satisfied smile to both guests. In the past few years there had been several quiet evenings where Werner had shared a drink or two with Philipa but the chemistry between them was such that it had a habit of becoming a maudlin affair. Too much loss on both sides, they had concluded. It always pleased him to see Philipa laughing.

Dessert was a course that all professed to have no room for. The arrival of a cream-and-chocolate cake smelling strongly of black cherries and kirsch liqueur proved irresistible. The cake was squeezed in, but now they were full beyond belief, sated with food and alcohol. Werner set a schnapps glass down in front of each diner and gained a reluctant assent to the pouring of the liquor. Some minutes later, on rising to locate the gents, George had to steady himself on a bust of Beethoven. He walked with a determined slowness towards the toilet, trying for the straight line that all those under the influence judge appropriate, but following instead a gentle parabola that was the best most guests could achieve.

Before they knew it the meal was over, Werner was embracing them both, they were thanking him and Dietrich in turn for a splendid evening. And so, Philipa and George found themselves on the pavement.

"Mr Bradfield, you are a very bad influence on me" slurred a squiffy Philipa Arden.

"I blame the Germans" countered an equally inebriated George, laughing heartily at a joke that wasn't there. For no reason Philipa laughed too.

"We are a disgrace" he concluded. Philipa regained her composure and stood up correctly.

"Now Mr Bradfield, I will have to find my way home and hope that no cad takes advantage of me in my weakened state."

"I would be happy to oblige" offered George, his usual courtesy returning.

"In terms of walking me home or taking advantage of me?" But before George could clarify Philipa held out her hand and they walked arm in arm towards the Arden residence. It was a short walk that neither of them would remember in the morning, but presently they found themselves at the door to Philipa's town house. At the top of the steps Philipa delved into her slim handbag looking for the door keys, George backed away a little to give her the benefit of the street lighting, but knocked something over with his foot. There was a fraction of a second of silence, gravity silently imparting an acceleration of 32 feet per second per second to the object, before a loud sound of breaking glass announced itself many feet below him. A single dog barked, and then another barked in answer, which led to a symphony of vulpine howls from across the neighbourhood. Philipa had now got the door opened and they removed themselves swiftly from the scene, giggling like school children.

George was seated on a sofa whilst Philipa busied herself preparing a pot of tea. He stared around the room morosely, higher brain functions disabled by the excesses of the evening. He took in the bookshelves and the prints, but didn't analyze their contents. Philipa returned with the tea pot and by an act of supreme concentration poured two cups out. They sat next to each other,

Philipa resting her head upon his shoulder, her left hand across his belly. George moved his own left arm around her. In a matter of minutes they were both asleep and would be until morning.

The Engineers

During the journey George felt uneasy and arriving at Doncaster he continued to have a bad feeling about the proposed meeting. George had been careful to make Stanier aware of the trip although he had explained it rather narrowly, and somewhat inaccurately, as a further exploration of the phenomena Jacob had demonstrated. He had been careful not mention the Night Watch nor the charms of Mrs Arden. It was now some weeks since his evening with her in Chester. Though the night had promised much it had ultimately ended inconclusively and they had parted the next morning with an icy kiss that lacked all intimacy. George grappled with the truth that she would forever be Second Lieutenant Alfred Arden's girl.

Mrs Arden met him off the York train. It was pulled by a single streamlined loco, elegant and curvaceous. They walked through the station hall, hailed a cab and were driven a short distance to the LNER loco works. George was uncertain how they would announce themselves. He felt like a spy operating behind enemy lines, however Mrs Arden walked smartly up to the receptionist and declared "Mr Bradfield and Mrs Arden, we have an appointment with Mr Maxwell". The receptionist smiled and suggested they take a seat.

They surveyed the leather sofas. They were a deeply unpleasant shade of light brown. George recalled stepping on something of a similar colour in Victoria Park the previous Sunday and remembered Mrs Minshull had not been impressed when he further trod it into the hall carpet. The sofas were seemingly rather wide, so George and Mrs Arden sat down on the same sofa. It turned out the sofas were so sprung as to push the two of them together. Lift and separate, only in reverse. Though it felt improper, George rather enjoyed such close contact with Mrs Arden. She smiled in an unfathomably way and looked into the middle distance. George adjusted his trousers and placed his attaché case across his lap.

Presently Mr Maxwell appeared and rather nervously shook both their hands. Mr Maxwell was a thin, rather unimpressive looking man of similar height to George. He smiled broadly and George felt rather more at ease. For some reason George had expected the

LNER to be staffed by a master race and he found considerable comfort in the ordinariness of their host. They were led through a maze of corridors smelling alternately of paper, ink, disinfectant and industrial lubricants. The journey terminated in a moderately large room on the first floor, overlooking a set of engine sheds. Mr Maxwell was joined by his assistant, Nicholas, a jovial character of similar proportions to his master.

"Welcome to Doncaster. It's really good to see you again Philipa..." said Maxwell. George hadn't yet got out of the habit of calling her Mrs Arden and rearranged his face at such informalities.

"...and welcome to our friend from the wrong side of the Pennines." Cheeky b----- thought George, but smiled. Whilst he wanted to be hostile, he couldn't help but like Maxwell.

The pleasantries continued for some minutes with Mr Maxwell and Mrs Arden enjoying a certain chemistry that lit an irrational, jealous fire within George. They were served with tea in a fine china service daubed in rather vulgar LNER emblems. Presently they got down to business.

"I understand you'd like to talk about the Goldsmith process" continued Maxwell. The Goldsmith process. That gave it an air of respectability previously lacking from Jacob's demonstration.

"If you mean the process that Samuel and Jacob Goldsmith have been working on, yes."

"What do you think of it?" enquired Maxwell

"I have no good explanation for it. At least no scientific one. It's intriguing. It can at least be reproduced but I'm reserving judgement. Jacob was very reluctant to give any specifics, even on the chemical composition of the salts he used. I think there's the possibility it's all smoke and mirrors."

"We thought the same. All seemed a bit "City of Truro"" replied Maxwell. George recognised the allusion, whilst Mrs Arden looked mystified.

"The Great Western engine "City of Truro" allegedly exceeded 100 miles an hour forty-odd years ago, but the proof was rather shaky" he added in explanation.

"Boys!" huffed Mrs Arden.

"It was only once we built our own equipment that we were satisfied we weren't being conned. Just as well. By then the Goldsmith family had got three thousand pounds out of us."

"You..." George reeled at the sudden onslaught of information.

"When I saw the process at their lab I was very suspicious. It looked like a hoax. But I knew it was worth more investigation, so I bought half their supply of salt off them and rigged up the same experiment here. Old Sam doesn't talk much about anything, whilst Jacob would talk about anything but the specifics of the process. I don't particularly care about the science behind it as long as it reliably raises steam. Turns out all you need to do is mix the salt with the water in a big enough quantity and off it goes."

"So you've run the experiment here in Doncaster?" asked George.

"Oh we've done a lot more than run the experiment!" Answered Maxwell's assistant. Maxwell looked sharply at his assistant but then broke into a smile.

"Would you like to see our latest research efforts, Mr Bradfield?"

"You bet!" replied George.

They stepped across a number of railway tracks, looking rather out of place amongst the fitters and firemen, and worked over towards a separate engine shed. The main entrance was shut up by a large wooden door and they penetrated the shed through a smaller door within the larger one. It took them a few seconds for their eyes to adjust to the reduced light in the shed, but presently the shape of a Locomotive emerged in front of them. It was similar to the one that had pulled George into Doncaster - an A4 Pacific - but was decorated in Silver rather than mid-blue. Steam hissed from the usual places, but the vent in the Engine shed roof was shut and the chimney of the Loco produced no smoke. Maxwell proudly announced:

"Ladies and Gentlemen, I present "The Republic of Great Britain"."

There were puzzled looks on the faces of George and Mrs Arden, Maxwell looked at his assistant for support then began

"Seemed like a good idea at the time, caught the spirit of the moment in late ‘thirty six. We keep getting pestered to change it - either to "Puffin" or name it after one of the directors." He shrugged as if there were a number of more important changes requiring his attention.

"Is this powered by what I think it's powered by?" ventured George.

"Certainly is - Steam" answered Maxwell's assistant glibly. They were both clearly enjoying their moment, but George was starting to tire of the music hall routine.

"What I meant was how are you heating the steam."

"The Goldsmith process."

"Can you raise as much steam as using coal?" enquired George.

"And the rest, We'd have to use best Welsh anthracite to raise the same amount this chap can raise." George was impressed, but also brooded again over the fact the LNER had got hold of this first.

"She's a beautiful sight, have you had her out on the main-line?" enquired Mrs Arden.

"Yes, though so far we've only had her out at night. The management don't know what to do with her. We could do a speed attempt and probably push the record up above 130, but we'd likely damage the big ends." He broke for comic effect but there was none to be had. Maxwell continued:

"..and it would be a lot of unwelcome publicity. There's talk of fitting her with some kind of smoke box to reduce suspicions, but nobody seems willing to make a decision." Maxwell looked at his feet again.

"There's also some talk of getting the Admiralty involved. Despite the Goldsmith's insistence on keeping this private. You can imagine this would be very useful on submarines or capital ships. I really doubt we can keep this secret for any length of time, and it would not suit our purpose for the Reichsbahn to get their hands on this." Maxwell sounded deflated now.

George was walking up and down the loco. He was full of awe at the sight of the loco, and Maxwell's team had done a first class job of adapting the Goldsmith process. George couldn't help but be envious. He drew little comfort from the fact the LNER was now in just as much of a muddle as the LMS had been when presented with the idea.

"Do you want to go up on the foot plate?" asked Maxwell.

"Yes please" replied George and Mrs Arden in unison.

They went out for lunch - Roast Beef, Yorkshire Puddings, Roast Potato and boiled Greens. Mrs Arden played safe with a Gin and Tonic whilst George sampled the Bitter. The head left a series of rings down the side of the glass indicating George's progress. Maxwell was emphasising a point by waving a piece of Yorkshire pudding around on the end of his fork.

"I understand Philipa has told you about the Night Watchman conspiracy." Mrs Arden's nose wrinkled at the word "conspiracy". She constantly found herself dispelling any idea that she was proposing a conspiracy, particularly amongst the true believers such as Mr Maxwell.

"I'm still very unclear." George cleared his throat. He liked the LNER chaps, saw them as kindred spirits, so he was comfortable enough to give it to them straight. "To tell you the truth, I only came here because Mrs...Philipa...promised I'd learn more about the Goldsmith process. I'm not very political, can't really be bothered with all the left and right stuff and I certainly can't be bothered with foreign matters."

"Then you have passed our most important criteria and I welcome you into the Night Watchman." Maxwell extended his hand in a comradely manner. George looked puzzled and turned to Mrs Arden, who in turn urged Maxwell to elaborate further.

"We get our name from the notion of a "night watchman state", that is a nation state that does only the minimum required to maintain society. A night watchman state provides police and armed forces and a justice system, but that is about it. It doesn't do public works, or get caught up in industry or agriculture. It leaves all that to its citizens, who, so the theory goes, know how best to get those things done."

"Sounds pretty similar to the old Whigs to me, all a bit outdated" said George who regretted immediately making any reference to politics.

"Well there are some similarities, but this is an even older idea, let me give you some history." This is what George had feared, but Maxwell was getting into his stride now. Mrs Arden had rather sensibly plucked a nail file out of her handbag and was performing running repairs to her elegant talons. Maxwell's assistant, Nicholas, was talking with the landlords blooming daughter over the bar

"The Night Watch goes back at least to the early 17th century. There are those that suggest it is named, somewhat tongue-in-cheek, after the night watchman in Act 2 Scene 3 of Macbeth."

"Equivocators" shouted Mrs Arden, whilst still paying fullest attention to her nails she giggled at her own joke. Nobody else understood. "And anyway it's a Porter in Macbeth" she added. Maxwell would not be deflected.

He elaborated. He told of Whigs and liberals of the big and little "L" variety. There were republicans and revolutionaries. The American republic got a mention, the pursuit of happiness was celebrated and the consent of the governed was agreed upon as a good thing. George truly regretted giving Maxwell any encouragement. Maxwell slowed down slightly and George caught up.

"Indeed membership wasn't something you applied for, you were approached. The theory being anybody who actively sought to join was fundamentally unsuited to membership" quoted Maxwell as he stopped to take a swig of his pint, George did the same. He felt like he ought to ask a question but no sensible one was forthcoming. Across the room the landlord's daughter laughed loudly, leaned forward in merriment and George caught an eyeful of her ample cleavage. He looked at Mrs Arden who was already looking at him. George blushed but Maxwell didn't notice and resumed the sermon.

Now it was the turn of the industrial revolution. George was treated to Maxwell's thoughts on guilds, unions, mill owners and sundry industrialists. George's ears pricked up at the mention of anarchists because even the violent overthrow of society had to be better than this unwelcome political education. But it was only a temporary relief. George's face gave away the fact his mind was forming a question.

"I just don't understand what they, or you, hope to achieve. It doesn't sound like you offer your members anything. Do you stand up for them like the trade unions do?"

"No, we maintain our security through stealth. Seek us and you can be sure not to find us. But we have no secrets. We exist to help one another, however we can. We exist as an alternative to a coercive power. We are a cooperative, in the broadest sense."

Mrs Arden had finished attending to her nails and silenced Maxwell with a simple look. She breathed deeply, commanding a pause in the conversation, and then spoke a full two seconds later.

"What Mr Maxell glosses over is that his story is mere conjecture. What we do know is it is most accurately described as "The Night Watchman" not the Night Watchmen or the Night Watch.

The truth is we don't know the history of the Night Watchman. We can surmise from informal histories that they or it originated some hundreds of years ago. We don't know with any certainty their reason for existing. It may be this rather liberal, hands-off approach to government is what they're all about. Or it may be something completely different. I have spoken with nobody who could disprove the fact they aren't just some fiction of the last few years. What I do know is there are clutches of individuals across the country with this rather odd belief. I got involved because it interested me as folklore. The problem is that once you get involved you start seeing coincidence and conspiracy everywhere. You must remember it's not a secret society, indeed it's not even much of a society. Its founding principal seems to be based on individuals helping one another. It was in that spirit that you were invited across the Pennines. I suppose it's quite worthy and certainly fairly harmless, though I wonder at its relevance."

Maxwell looked rather put out. Mrs Arden realised she may have upset him. She mulled over what she could say to smooth his ruffled feathers.

"I'm not suggesting you aren't sincere. I think you chaps are splendid fellows. I enjoy our little conspiracies, but let's not give Mr Bradfield any false impression of what we know."

Maxwell continued to look rather crestfallen.

"Where does Inspector Francis Kaye come into this?" asked George.

"I don't know exactly" replied Mrs Arden. "But he certainly seems very interested in the Night Watchman. I have a few friends in the Metropolitan Police, but none of them has been able to tell me what Inspector Kaye does. If I had to guess I would say he investigates political organisations, though in what capacity and to what end I do not know."

"The point of today is to welcome you into our little group" said Maxwell. "Don't worry, I'll not talk politics with you again. But I'm happy to talk about engineering over another pint."

"That sounds like the best idea this lunchtime" remarked George. He rose to get to the bar and buy a round of drinks.

And so we leave this Yorkshire conspiracy in "The Volunteer" public house, Doncaster. George stands nervously at the bar trying to catch the landlords eye as the lunchtime rush draws to a close.

Maxwell and Mrs Arden are engaged now in a fervent debate about the accuracy of historical sources. Nicholas, Maxwell's demon, is now fully engaged in a bawdy conversation with the landlord's daughter that becomes more disordered with time.

Meeting Rosa

George was returning from his meeting with the Night Watchman. For all that he had learnt it had been an unsatisfactory meeting, not only confirming his own ignorance, but holding little hope of any further enlightenment. Now it was just coming up to 4 in the afternoon of a hot and stifling afternoon. George had been wearing his suit jacket as the easiest means of carrying it, with the result that he had sweated profusely whilst waiting for the train home from York. Now boarding the train he wished he had left it off. The train was not busy, so he found an empty compartment in which to re-arrange himself. He removed the jacket and stowed it with his holdall. He sat awkwardly, allowing his cotton shirt to dry on his frame. The air in the carriage was still and hot, with the smell of old seat upholstery. George wished he had got a paper or magazine for the long journey back to Crewe. He toyed with the idea of darting out to the news stand on the platform, but feared the train was about to leave. He was confirmed in this suspicion as the whistle blew and the train lurched forwards. George stood up to get a couple of sheets of paper from his bag and a pencil. Scribbling random thoughts would have to do, at least until Leeds.

Just as the train cleared the platform the door to the compartment was opened. Though there was no good reason, George half expected it to be Mrs Arden. It was not. Instead there stood briefly in the door way a woman in her mid to late twenties. She was short, about five foot, and wore a beaming smile.

"Excuse me, love, are these seats taken?" she asked in an accent George struggled to place. His struggle, which took him from the Mersey to the Thames and then to the Tyne held him tongue tied, so the new arrival had to nod her head in the direction of the seats, as if repeating the question.

"Yes, eh, no". "They're free" George said inconclusively. By some miracle of non-verbal communication the young lady had managed to understand George, and sat down. She then realised she hadn't put her bags away. George, realising this too, offered help and lifted them onto the rack above the seats. He reflected on the fact this pleasant young woman would get an unpleasant view of his still damp shirt. For her part, the young woman was just glad to sit down.

"George Bradfield" he said as he offered his hand. She shook it with a fleshy but delicate hand. George sat down on the seats opposite and he realised that "fleshy but delicate" would be a perfect description for this new entrant to the compartment.

"Rosa Consett" replied the young woman. George was still unable to place the accent either by geography or class. The name Rosa sounded rather foreign. "My Dad says I'm called after Rosa Luxemburg" George was none the wiser. "My Mum says she just liked the name." She was still smiling as she surveyed the dull, sun bleached landscape through the window.

After five minutes Rosa stood up and fetched a modest glass bottle from within her bag. It contained a bright, carbonated green liquid which fizzed loudly as she opened it.

"Would you like some Cream Soda?" asked Rosa. To prolong the conversation George said yes. He was expecting her to fetch a second bottle out of the bag, but instead she took a long sip from the bottle and passed it to George. A product of the middle class George felt uneasy about drinking from another's bottle, but also felt it would be rude to refuse and ruder still to wipe the bottle. He took a cautious draft from the bottle. It was warm and tasted vaguely of vanilla ice cream. Far from providing refreshment the sugary liquid caused an immediate thirst. But he smiled and thanked Rosa as he passed the bottle back. She smiled too.

"Where are you going to?" asked Rosa.

"Crewe" replied George "How about you?"

"Liverpool."

"Is that where you live?"

"For the next two weeks, then I'm off to Birmingham, then probably Manchester."

Answers that prompted more questions. George was reminded of the previous day. But Rosa had got in her stride now. George only needed to provide the vaguest encouragement and Rosa would provide a fulsome answer. A nod here, an "oh yes?" there and they proceeded in happy dialog. George felt oddly at ease in her company.

"I work for Gathurst's" announced Rosa.

"The clothing store?" George recalled a branch opening in Crewe shortly before Christmas, with much fanfare. It had undercut every local clothes store. George had bought the suit he was wearing today from there. It was half the price of anywhere else and looked rather smart from ten foot away. Closer scrutiny revealed it to be rather cheap. The closest scrutiny would reveal that the pockets had come unstitched and were now held together by numerous staples from the LMS stationary cupboard. George had been rather pleased with this improvisation, until he realised he had left a sixpence rattling around in the hem.

"The very same. Have you ever had anything from them?" Rosa knew the answer from the smile on George's face.

"My outfit's from there too. It's worth every penny!" laughed Rosa.

"What do you do at Gathursts?"

"I'm what they call a merchandiser. I advise how to set out the stock. What to put in the windows. How to get the most sales." George could see she was proud of her job.

"My dad says it's not a proper job and I just sit around a shop all day. But I spend most of the day standing and it's hard work."

"But you enjoy it?" asked George.

"Yes, I wanted to work with animals, but the customers are a good substitute."

They both laughed. The journey continued and they chatted amiably, with Rosa doing most of the talking and George providing the occasional encouragement. The cream soda bottle was finished by the time they got into Leeds. George darted out of the train and bought two further bottles of fizzy drinks, one a sulphurous yellow claiming to be orangeade, the other a dark brown dandelion and burdock. Rosa opened the dandelion and burdock and after taking a sip, passed it to George. In George's mind was the prospect that there was the short journey to Huddersfield and then Stalybridge where he had to change trains. Less than 1 further hour in Rosa's company. Maps of the railway network of North West England played through his mind. He was meant to get the train to Stockport, then change again for the train to Crewe. It was an awkward series of changes, but much the quickest route. By contrast Rosa would likely be staying on the train right through to Liverpool Lime Street, at least two hours distant. George conceived of the idea of staying on as far as Liverpool and then getting the train directly to Crewe. It was a long way round, but that was really the point. He made an excuse to Rosa about going to the toilet and sought out the guard. George was a cautious individual, so even as he made plans to prolong his time with Rosa, he wanted to ensure the ticketing was in order. The guard was a thin, gentlemanly Yorkshire man who couldn't understand why George wanted to pay additional money for a longer journey. George fumbled "I've just met a girl.." and the guard smiled a knowing smile, took George's money, patted him on the shoulder and wished him the best of British.

He returned to Rosa a few minutes later. The sun shone into the carriage and George had chance to take in her curves. A full bust and rear and a beautiful round elfin face illuminated by the late afternoon sun. She had finished the dandelion and burdock and was struggling with something. George looked at her with some concern.

"I love fizzy pop, but I can never burp without making a noise" confessed Rosa.

"Don't struggle on my account" offered George as he sat down.

A fog horn of a burp rang out, Rosa looked at first horrified and then couldn't suppress a fit of the giggles. George laughed too. After the mirth subsided Rosa looked towards George's pad of paper. A game of noughts and crosses was suggested and, as the dark satanic mills of Blake's Jerusalem rolled by they amused themselves in a mock competition. Huddersfield and Stalybridge came all too quickly, then Manchester and the train filled with commuters. But their conversation continued as they rattled across the Lancashire countryside, past coal mines and rubber works, past Rainhill and its historic trials and into the outskirts of Liverpool.

The train slowed now as it crawled through the approach tunnels to Lime Street. George looked at the blackened walls with their pick marks. Less than one hundred years ago navies toiled for months through bedrock so that I might get an extra few minutes with this lady opposite. But those minutes were running out and they both knew it. Presently George must find his train to Crewe and Rosa would have to find her guesthouse. They disembarked reluctantly, knowing the journey to be at an end now. George wondered by what pretext he could delay their parting but none presented itself. So they wished each other goodbye and good luck. George was about to turn when Rosa remarked:

"I get Sunday's off. Would you be able to show me around Liverpool?"

George only vaguely knew the city but leapt at this opportunity.

"I'd love to, I can show you the Cathedral and the Walker Gallery and...." his knowledge ran out at this point. But it didn't matter.

"Shall we meet here at half ten? In the morning?" ventured Rosa.

"I'll be here" said George. And he knew he would be. If he had to walk from Crewe, he'd be there. In his best suit. The one with the stapled pockets and the sixpence in the hem.

The Nightmare

George rolled over uneasily in his bed, trying to find a position of comfort in which to sleep but only succeeding in pulling the sheets further away from the bed. He was too burdened to sleep and if it wouldn't have woken Mrs Minshull, and brought on unwanted ministrations and quack remedies, he would have got up and read in the front room downstairs. In his head were various demons that had no right to be to the fore of his thoughts. He wanted to curl up and dream about the possibilities that meeting Rosa may now afford him. But instead he had in his mind the events of the preceding days. Prime amongst his fears was the thought that Inspector Kaye must know he had visited Doncaster and with whom. Simultaneously there lingered more vague concerns over the Goldsmith process, over what Maxwell and Nicholas would do with it, over how he and Stanier could have made more of it. And around the shipwreck of these anxieties swan shoals of minor doubts about work undone or bills unpaid. In desperation George tried a trick that had worked in the past. In this he considered all his doubts to be written on a suitably pliant piece of paper. He visualised rolling this up and tying it with a piece of handsome red ribbon. He then stored it in a dark recess of his mind, to be opened only when he wanted to. In the end he achieved a fitful sleep if only because he put his brain into a recursive loop trying to tie the knot in the ribbon.

The house was deathly quiet and the streets outside were still some hours away from being thronged with the first workers of the day. George's recursive loop found an exit condition and presently he found himself in Liverpool, or at any rate what looked like Liverpool. It was however a queer sort of Liverpool for walking around the corner into Bold Street deposited him instead in Manchester. George's mind noted this but did not think it particularly odd. A brief pause, perhaps the clock on the mantelpiece downstairs strikes three, and we register that we are indeed dreaming but allow the fiction to continue. By turns the city resolves more definitely into Manchester. The tram lines sing with the approach of a tram, but George notes now that it is not a tram. Instead it is one of the A4s of the LNER, dressed like "The

Republic of Great Britain" in a fine silver and black. It approaches now so slowly that we can run our hand along the curve of its shape, a rapid rise up the skirt and slow taper down again to the rear. The footplate approaches and we look up, but see no driver or fireman, only the dull blue glow through the sight glass – it is powered by the Goldsmith process. We pause to consider the implications. Has it achieved a form of independence from us, now that no one tends the regulator at its throat? When the source of power might last weeks or even months what is to stop this behemoth from enslaving us? The lines take it away from us and we catch our breath down a side street. Composure of a kind returns. Which way leads us out of this Manchester? Quickly now, for we can see another A4 passing a hundred yards away, slowing at the crossroads as if to stare down the alleyway in our direction. This one painted in an austere, not to say authoritarian, black. We run now, escaping from engines variously liveried in garter blue, light green, silver and the most fearsome of all the black leader. Strange to note, during our flight, that the city has changed once more. The buildings have become fewer, though no less grand. Rather in the style of the Victorian etchings of early railway infrastructure, which omitted the surroundings for clarity, we see vast plains surrounding Central station, all bathed in a golden sunlight. People, too, are sparse, represented only in a vague stick-like manner somewhere between a Lowry and Bruegel's "Triumph of Death". Is this the present or the past? Are we still being pursued by the LNER? Hard to say, but we take now a greater interest in the surroundings. We are being led by our Grandfather past the scenery of a contemporary city, but in places a building has been, seemingly, surgically removed and all that remains is a fraction of its masonry lying perfectly flat. What has wrought this immense but rather specific damage? A bombing plane or the now dormant A4s? We are told by our Grandfather that it was so many years ago, back when he was a vital young man. Except a doubt creeps into our mind – are we the Grandfather or the child? And presently our grip slips and the two are estranged. Forever. Tears burst forth, too long suppressed, running uncontrollably down our cheeks and we seek shelter in the arms of a Mother we thought we were too old for.

Millions are still asleep, some may indeed be dreaming of terrifying monsters. But George is awake, with only the dull ache of pins and needles in the index and forefinger for company.

When George arrived down for breakfast some hours later Mrs Minshull was already in the kitchen. From practice, she wordlessly sat George at the table and placed a bowl of cornflakes in front of him. A couple of weeks ago she had noticed George's nascent middle-age spread and switched from her fortifying morning fry-ups to grapefruit and the American cereals that had come into vogue some decades earlier.

"I saved you the cream from the milk" she chirped as she poured the milk into his bowl. George reached for the sugar bowl and sprinkled a tablespoonful across the cereal. The Minshull diet was unlikely to yield results any time soon.

As George was finishing his breakfast there was a knock on the door. The old lady was decanting last night's dripping into a jug, so George got up to answer it. The figure of Inspector Kaye stood in the middle of the path.

"Good Morning Mr Bradfield." George felt a deadweight where the cornflakes rested. Somehow he had known this moment was coming. He just hoped he could now spare Mrs Minshull too much embarrassment. There were, as yet, no net curtains twitching along the street. He invited the Inspector inside and asked to use the front room. Mrs Minshull eyed George with some suspicion and the Inspector with a certain indignation. How dare he bother the nice Mr Bradfield who, whatever depravity might be practiced out of her sight, at least paid the rent on time.

"I understand you met with our Mrs Arden recently" began the Inspector.

"I did" admitted George gloomily. This could be messy, thought George.

"I gather that this was a planned meeting."

"It was." Stick to the truth. Shame I didn't do that earlier, he brooded.

"Not very talkative this morning, George?"

"I'm sorry Inspector, I know I should have told you, I …." He had no excuse. It was a sin of omission, but it didn't make it any less of a sin.

"I don't believe you are either a fool or a conspirator. We can all have a blind spot when it comes to the fairer sex. However you said you would keep me informed of any further contact and I would like you to honour that pledge. I have had to expend resources I could have used much more profitably in following your antics these last few days." The Inspector stopped, there was a look upon his face suggesting he had said too much, but he was such a wily old hound this might just be part of his act. George remained silent, not strictly exercising any right to silence, more seeking refuge in it. The Inspector continued in a slightly different vain, rather annoyed that he was having to talk so much. Years in the job had proven that you were rarely in control of a conversation when you were talking. Much better to let the other man talk.

"Do you know the real difference between a democracy and a dictatorship, Mr Bradfield?" George looked at the Inspector in bewilderment. The Inspector continued.

"In a democracy a morning knock on the door is probably the postman, in a dictatorship it could be the secret police, and that element of doubt is a powerful control." George thought this through. In a democracy it could also be the rent man, the landlord or the bailiff, but George would settle for any of those right now. Did that make the Inspector a *secret* policeman. Did it make England a democracy or a dictatorship? The questions he would ask if only he dared.

"I am not a secret policeman. I am a humble detective inspector in the Met. It's my job to uphold the law and keep the peace. It is not my job to meter out justice or punishment. That is the job of real gentlemen in horse-hair wigs." George had never really appreciated this distinction, but was still fearful of where this was leading.

"I would like you to appreciate all this. I would also like you to understand what I can do. I could have you arrested and hold you in a police cell for a couple of days. I could appear at your front door again, maybe in a police car. That would get the neighbours talking, wouldn't it? I could turn up at your work, ask to speak with your superiors, make some crude insinuations along the same lines as my colleagues you met some months ago. On the other hand, I understand you met a charming young lady the other day. Rosa wasn't it? I could speak to her father. Perhaps you forced yourself upon her? I could speak with her employers and question the character of those she associates with. I could have her arrested. The problem with you revolutionaries and conspirators is what you hide. It might be necessary to have her undress, perform an intimate search. Front and back, so to speak. It would all be above board, WPC and Physician present. Legally tidy for me although deeply unpleasant for the poor girl."

"You can't do that!" exclaimed George.

"But I can, Mr Bradfield. Our democratic state limits my powers, but really the only thing that stops abuses is the good character of most of the constabulary."

"What do you want?" But George already knew before the Inspector answered.

"Only what you promised me the first night we met. The truth." The Inspector sat a little further forwards in his chair and brought his hands together as if in prayer. Over the next thirty minutes George gave a full and honest description of his trip to Doncaster. He spared nothing - his feelings for Mrs Arden, the jealousy and despair he felt when she seemed just as intimate with Maxwell, the details of the Goldsmith process, their discussions in the pub and his acquaintance with Rosa on the journey home. He had never really appreciated the relief that confession might bring. As a child of the Church of England he had always had a slight distaste for the ways of the Church of Rome. But, sat in Mrs Minshull's front room on a weekday morning, late for work and helping the police with their enquiries he had a damascene conversion, at least for a few minutes. As he was finishing his tale the Inspector brought it to an abrupt halt by closing his black notebook.

"Thank you." He seemed torn between a desire not to take any more of George's time and a feeling that there were some further words of wisdom he could pass on.

"I'm sorry we had to have the distasteful stuff, the threats, earlier." George wanted to say something but shrugged instead. There were vile trains of thought he would have to get out of his mind, but he bore the Inspector no ill will.

"I have spoken with Philipa Arden only once but I think I understand something of the attraction you feel to her. Add this to the rather obvious physical charms you have mentioned and it amounts to quite a spell. As a policeman I've come to understand a little about human nature. From what you say I cannot imagine you having any future together. I wouldn't presume to give you advice, but if I was in your shoes I would ignore this Mrs Arden and her Night Watchmen and enjoy every moment instead in the company of young Rosa."

George had been coming to a similar conclusion since the Doncaster trip and managed a weak smile.

"Well Mr Bradfield, I'll let you get on with your day." And that was it. No arrest. No threats. No requirement to keep him informed. The Inspector bid goodbye to Mrs Minshull, who appeared to have made herself very busy in the kitchen. She had clearly been listening in, but not sufficiently to get the whole picture so George then suffered a further interrogation, this time from his landlady. He told the same tale, in briefer form, aware that he was now very late for work. Mrs Minshull listened with all the rigor of the Inspector.

"I think the Inspector talks a lot of sense. That Rosa girl sounds like a nice sort. If you'd like to bring her back for tea one day I could do my summer pudding." George appreciated the offer, but felt it was a little early in the courtship to introduce her to Mrs Minshull's efforts at the classic seasonal dessert.

"I've known other young men to become infatuated with confident, older women. My experience is that such relationships can be enjoyable for both parties but don't lead anywhere" she observed authoritatively, whilst adjusting her pendulous bosom with her forearm. George laughed uneasily and left quickly for work.

Ginger Beer

Their reunion in Liverpool had been a triumph unfettered by any knowledge George might have thought he had of the city. After five minutes they were lost and after ten George admitted as much to a still cheerful Rosa. Instead they roamed as if they were Scott or Shackleton, discovering new delights round every corner, despite most shops and cafés being closed for the Sabbath. As the day drew to an end they parted company on Lime Street station again, this time agreeing to write to one another. George bent forwards and kissed Rosa gently on the lips. Years had proven George to be utterly inept at choosing the right moment to kiss a girl. He had seen this one kiss as a singular sign of affection, without being too overt or pushy. Rosa had hoped for more. She wondered if he felt for her as she did for him. Or was this the end of another what-might-have-been romance? She resolved that if he wrote to her sincerely in the next few days he was just shy, whereas if it was the end of the week before he wrote she could assume it would amount to nothing.

She was not to be disappointed for George wrote her a charming note on the train home. It was rather lacking in presentation (written on cheap lined notebook paper in an unsteady hand made worse by the movement of the train) but it came from the heart. Rosa, duly charmed, was thrilled when George proposed a trip to the zoo.

Rosa was now working in Manchester and they met at Piccadilly Station, journeying out to Belle Vue on an overcrowded local service. As the initial thrill of being reunited subsided Rosa turned the conversation onto George's brush with the law. It was curious, she reflected, how she had reacted to this news. With most men it would have made her distinctly wary. But there had been something remarkably disarming about the manner in which George had announced the details. He had seemed so forlorn in mentioning it, so certain that it would taint their relationship that she accepted it at face value, for there could be no faking such distress. Now, some weeks after hearing of it, Rosa was rather tickled by the prospect of George being in trouble with the police. It seemed so thoroughly unlikely.

"Have you had any more visits from Inspector Kaye?"

"No, thankfully" responded George rather flatly.

"I think it's all a bit thrilling this business of being under surveillance. It's like something from one of those stories in my magazine" she tapped a trashy title that was poking out of her handbag.

"It's all a bit of a bore to be honest, especially since I'm an innocent man."

"You're not thinking like a secret policeman, love. Try to use your imagination. We're all guilty of something." She said smiling knowingly, and then blushed as if remembering a heinous crime she was guilty of. George smiled his own goofy grin and decided he'd play the game.

"So Miss Consett, what vile deed have you perpetrated?" He put on his best policeman's voice, all authority and adenoids.

"You'll never get it out of me, you, you ... lackey of the bourgeoisie!" she squeaked back.

""Lackey of the bourgeoisie" which 19th century anarchists den have you crept out of?"

"My Dad was always shouting it at the newspaper."

"Ah, of course. I forgot you are Frauline Rosa Luxembourg."

"I'll take your word for it. I didn't choose this name. But if I'm going to be Rosa Guttenburg.."

"Luxembourg" he corrected

"If I'm going to be Rosa Luxembourg, then you will have to be my comrade in arms."

"Of course. Let me think" and George racked his brain for a heroic revolutionary name.

"I will be Nikolai Bukharin."

"Never heard of him, but it sounds exotic."

"He was executed by the NKVD earlier this year."

"Oh George! This is meant to be fun."

"Sorry."

"I'll let you off, this time" she chided him "So, we are Nikolai and Rosa, two desperate revolutionaries bent on the overthrow of a wicked and corrupt system that has enslaved the world in the pursuit of money"

"I'm starting to have my doubts about you. Does old man Gathurst know he has a red working for him?"

"Remember, this is just a game my love?"

"So what are we going to do?"

"We are going to blend in as humble tourists, visitors to the Belle Vue Zoological Gardens." She cracked a cheeky grin looking up from under her fringe.

"We shall take their bread and circuses and use them as weapons in the fight for the emancipation of the proletariat!" proclaimed George.

"Something like that" said Rosa "As long as I get to see the animals."

"And you will, of course, have to maintain our cover by treating me to all the indulgences a decadent shop-girl would expect from a day at the zoo."

"Really?" answered George with mock-weariness.

"Oh yes. Otherwise I'll tell Inspector Kaye."

Walking from the railway station to the zoo, their first sight of Belle Vue left them both rather awed. An enormous rollercoaster towered over the landscape, whilst at ground level they observed the steady flow of people entering the amusement park and fluorescent posters highlighting current and forthcoming attractions. Rosa looked around with a naive wonder.

"We never had time to come to places like this when I was a girl." She looked at George, as if making a confession. "We never had the money, come to that."

"It's been a long time since I came here. Probably fifteen, twenty years" admitted George, now made conscious of his retreating youth.

It was true there had been little spare time or money in Rosa's childhood. She held Belle Vue Zoo in the same regard as the Empire State Building or the RMS Queen Mary - potent symbols of the modern world. And if this modern world, with its meals of bread-and-margarine and intermittent aroma of chlorate bleach wasn't perfect, well it was at any rate better than her pre-history of eking out an existence on an isolated farm.

George, who had enjoyed a more affluent childhood and had a certain cynicism of commercial entertainment, marvelled instead at the engineering. Here, thought George, amongst concrete and Bakelite, to the tune of an ever present loud speaker we are entertained, whether we like it or not. What struck him wasn't the modernity of the place, for it was unremarkable in appearance and he knew it had stood for at least fifty years. Rather, it was the ease with which it seemed to have assimilated to each passing year. One hundred years from now, he mused, this place will doubtless still stand, entertaining future generations with contrivances of wood, steel and electric motors that will seem to light the way to the ever distant future.

Whilst Rosa trilled with delight at the sheer variety of the attractions, George reached into his jacket, his fingers closing around the reassuring bulk of florins and half crowns. He was going to enjoy today and damn the expense. They ambled into the grounds and examined the map. The main purpose of the day was visiting the animals, and Rosa was not shy in communicating the urgent necessity of this. Nonetheless their gaze inevitably wandered to the scenic railway, the enormous boating lake, the skating rink and the exotic tearooms, restaurants and even a Chinese café.

The late morning passed rapidly in the zoo proper. Rosa skipped from pachyderm to ungulate to primate and thence to marsupials and rodents before taking a nervous, reluctant tour around the reptile house. With commendable disdain for scientific conventions she employed her own system of taxonomy which rated the animal life by three simple dimensions – cuddly, smelly and scary. George decided not to ask where he fell within this spectrum.

Their appetite for animal life satisfied for the moment, the pair walked hand-in-hand around the other attractions. The sun had burnt off what little cloud there was and jackets were being shed and sleeves rolled up. In the confusion of removing layers and mopping perspiration they were apprehended by someone imploring them to visit a clairvoyant and before either could protest they were ushered through into a shaded booth and seated in front of a woman wearing a loose fitting cotton dress in a striking shade of imperial purple.

"It's two bob for one of you or I'll do the both of you for half a crown" she said with a professional weariness. It was the age-old voice of the jaded harlot, joylessly performing one more service.

"That's pricey. Aren't you meant to say "cross my palm with silver" or something like that?" queried Rosa with some defiance.

"Since they started adulterating the coinage with copper and nickel I find it's better to be precise, my love. I'll tell you what – I'll read the cards for the both of you for one and six as long as you promise not tell anyone."

"It's a deal" said Rosa, content she had struck a bargain and looking now at George who reached reluctantly into his pocket. He had a suspicion of clairvoyants, mediums and other pedlars of phenomena that weren't subject to rigorous scientific proof, but he bit his tongue. The woman took his money and placed it into a bowl of other coins, mostly sixpences.

They were treated to what is called a "cold reading". Whether the woman possessed any psychic abilities remained unproven, but she was an accomplished thespian, slipping comfortably into a character that in a less tolerant age would likely have landed her on the ducking stool. She started with some general statements covering their recent past which after some pressing Rosa and George agreed roughly fitted their circumstances. She made a couple of assertions which didn't strike home but moved quickly on. At least once she pushed Rosa to think hard how a statement might apply to her:

"Please my dear, it is important."

"I'm sorry but I don't know anyone called Nigel."

"How about Nigeria? Do you have any family in West Africa?"

"I had an Uncle who worked in the Merchant Navy" admitted Rosa.

"Yes, well it's all connected" insisted the woman.

Neither Rosa nor George dared ask the only question that either was really interested in. Whatever her other talents, the Clairvoyant had divined this within a few minutes. She smiled inwardly as she delivered her most important prediction, maintaining a solemn outward appearance she concluded:

"Although you have only recently met, you already have a special bond and can look forward to a long future together." Rosa and George smiled sweetly, neither keen to admit their excitement to the other, both rather embarrassed that their own question should have been answered in this fulsome, if unsolicited, manner. The Clairvoyant allowed herself a thin smile. As a prediction it was certainly possible she was wrong, but she knew young love when she saw it and sometimes it just needed a gentle prod from the hand of fate.

After lunch they relaxed on the lawn, the afternoon sun having now a fierceness which they tolerated if only because it was such a novelty. A single cloud floated slowly across the sky, white and fluffy, as if made from finely spun candy floss. George took aim at it with his rolled up umbrella and gently squeezed off a shot. He blew air through his lips and allowed the umbrella to recoil, mimicking the dispatch of a real projectile into the heavens. Rosa giggled and passed the ginger beer bottle across to him. He took a draft and suppressed a shudder from the effervescence.

"Just a warning shot. He'll think twice before raining on us" concluded George.

"I'm glad you left him still floating around. He is quite a pretty cloud."

George looked at her and smiled tenderly. Rosa stroked a strand of hair back from her face and tucked it behind her ear. George leant forward and kissed her, breaking off after a few seconds. They embraced instead and exchanged small talk. Rosa turned the conversation back to the visit of Inspector Kaye. She found the whole thing highly amusing and kept chuckling at the prospect of George as a fugitive from justice.

"It's all rather embarrassing"

"Oh I don't know. I think it's quite exciting. Imagine being a real revolutionary!"

"Your namesake would probably agree"

"Who?"

"Rosa Luxembourg."

"Oh her. To be honest I don't really know that much about the other Rosa."

"Have you never been tempted to find out?"

"Not really. It's not like we're related is it? I know she was some French politician or something, but that's about it. You're the first person I've ever met who'd actually heard of her."

"She was a bit of a figurehead in the sort of company I kept at University."

"Tell me about her?" asked Rosa, incurious but aware that George was keen to expand on the subject.

"She was German, not French. She was also a Marxist. When the Great War broke out she was active in the peace movement, which in the Kaiser's Germany was enough to get her locked up."

"That's brave, although not very clever."

"Quite. But that's not all. In prison she wrote a number of books, including one critical of the Russian revolution."

"Typical lefty. The only thing they like doing more than criticising the rest of us is criticising each other" observed Rosa, rather proud of such an insight.

"It is a talent that left-wing movements seem to have" admitted a slightly amused George before continuing.

"In any case, when the war ended she was one of the leaders of the German socialists. She stood up for what she believed in, and resisted the clamp down that came when the revolutions in Germany failed. In the end they shot her."

"Who? The Nazis?" asked Rosa.

"God no. It can't have been later than 1920, well before Hitler and co. I suppose it was their forerunners, the Freikorps or someone" George rubbed his nose. Had he done her justice?

"She sounds like quite a lady" said Rosa.

"I dare say she was. But the thing I like best about her was the fact she was one of the awkward squad. She once said that true freedom is the freedom to disagree." They were both quiet for a moment, silent in their thoughts as they observed the single fluffy cloud floating slowly to the east.

"I'm not sure I fancy being shot, but I still think it would be exciting being a revolutionary. You have to admit it would be a giggle? I could be the figurehead. I've got the name and I've got the looks."

"I dread to think what trouble you could drag me into, but I'm sure it would be great fun" admitted George.

Broken

“Eighty Three” shouted Stickland, eyes moving only from his stop watch to his pad of paper and then back to the window in expectation of the next mile post. George had before him a set of one-inch-to-the-mile maps covering the area from Norton Bridge to Crewe. Eighty three miles an hour and they hadn’t quite topped Whitmore summit. The others in the carriage allowed a thin smile over their scowls of grim concentration. They were also measuring the speed, or busying them with tasks relevant to the record attempt. In truth it now came down to how well the fireman could feed coal into the firebox and how efficiently the driver could use the steam so generated.

George looked up from the map and caught the eye of the man from the press office.

“Looking good” whispered the press man. George returned a sceptical stare.

“Not bad” George answered quietly.

“Are you engineers always such a cheery bunch?”

George looked back at his maps. There really wasn’t anything he could do. Even at Euston he’d felt like a spare part. The driver and fireman had humoured him as he briefed them on the boiler design, but they didn’t need to know about the details of heat transfer and carnot cycles. Their world was one of intuition and experience. They would have their own feel for the engine and make their decisions based on a wealth of minor details. Even though he marvelled at this, George would never truly understand such an empathetic approach.

“Smile, it might never happen” urged the press man “The name’s Gramsci, by the way, Tony Gramsci.”

“Bradfield, George Bradfield.”

“Pleased to meet you George. It’s a cracking little raceway this stretch” continued Tony.

”It’s too close to Crewe station really, but it’s about the best we have.”

“There’s plenty of space, isn’t there?” enquired Gramsci waving his hand over the maps.

"The approach to Crewe is restricted to 25 mile an hour, and for good reason. We'll have to cross three sets of points, any one of which could derail us much above 30."

"Christ, you're a barrel of laughs aren't you?" Duly shamed, George smiled, and realised he was indulging himself.

"We should be able to get up to about hundred and ten before we have to brake." He replied in a more cheery tone.

"We need one fourteen for the record." The press office man looked anxious.

"I'm sure the driver will bend the laws of physics as best he can." If anyone could foil the constraints of Newtonian mechanics, it was an LMS engine driver, thought George. His eyes returned to the map. They would have to start braking just after Chorlton. If they left it as late as Basford they were in real trouble. If they reached the marshalling yards before braking then platforms 1 to 6 would be decorated in the remains of Caledonian blue coaches.

"If it's such a tight run thing it's a shame we built the station where we did."

"Well that's one of the great "What-Ifs"" conceded George.

"I'm serious. If we do top one fourteen today, it's only a start. The competition will be on our tails. What do we do when the record gets above one twenty?"

"Give up chasing glory and go back to operating railways?" suggested George.

"Ninety!" shouted somebody. There was a ripple of approval and then a hush, as if any second somebody would shout out another significant speed. Instead it was a tortuous few minutes before a time keeper indicated they were making one hundred miles an hour.

"Could we move the station?" asked Gramsci.

"Just for today?" asked George, rolling his eyes.

"No, but in the next few years? Or even just change the track alignment? Indulge me. I'm just trying to think laterally."

"You're asking the wrong person, but I would say no chance. You're hemmed in by the Shrewsbury and Stoke lines to the South and the Chester and Manchester lines to the North."

In fact the LMS was the victim of circumstance and intransigence. When the Grand Junction Railway had initially proposed a station, a century ago, the first choice had been Nantwich, the second choice was Winsford with Crewe a poor third. Local landowners in the first two had dug in their heels and so Crewe (population: 70) had been the unlikely victor. In 1837 the requirement for many miles of flat, straight track for racing trains at one hundred twenty miles an hour had been a distant prospect.

"One Seven."

"Looks like we'll comfortably beat your hundred and ten."

George was silent. The motion of the train felt different now. Of course above ninety the streamlining would actually be of use, rather than the three tons of upturned bath-tub it was most of the time. But the change George noticed wasn't about airflow, it was harsher, more percussive. Every bump and imperfection in the track was picked up, the carriages were held taut by the still accelerating engine, but what would happen when they applied the brakes? He looked at his maps, they were just passing Madeley.

"One ten" Everybody was now waiting for the next measurement. It would be 30-odd seconds to the next mile post.

"One ten again." There were curses throughout the carriage and then the look of the inveterate gambler when he's staked his last half crown on a sure tip, willing his nag on. Another half minute of silence.

"One eleven."

"I have it as one twelve."

"Me too" shouted Stickland as they sped past Betley Mere. Gramsci was rubbing his hands together now and silently mouthing "Come on you beauty". George looked out of the train at the passing fields, a dapple grey mare paused from her hay and stared at the passing train as if enquiring what their business was and why they had disturbed her routine. It was a brief, curious window into the past. But the 20th Century would not be silent for long. The familiar clackerty-clack of the train was giving way to a less serene sound - a serious of hammer blows every time they passed from one rail to the next across the thermite weld.

The timers had now started making half-mile measurements, desperate to catch the peak speed. Conversation was muted. George looked once again at the map. Another thirty seconds and they would surely have to brake, wouldn't they? He looked once more out of the window and counted down. As he got to twenty eight seconds Chorlton flashed by, but there was no sign of the brakes.

"One fourteen."

"Confirmed. One fourteen" said another timer. Another ripple of excitement, but it wasn't over yet. Dare they hope for still faster? The official timers were keeping quiet, tending to their own, more sophisticated apparatus, and unwilling to make snap pronouncements. George looked at the map and then the green landscape whizzing by. Perhaps another twenty seconds and they would pass Basford Hall. And then what? Should he pull the communication cord? Another measurement, some confusion this time, the timer's nerves were shot as much as George's were. Estimates ranged from one twelve to one fourteen. They passed the second-to-last bridge before Basford, time and distance compressed. George recalled a text book that had tried to explain the theory of relativity to him. There had been pictures of elongated people on station platforms weighing twice their weight, the clock showing only half the true time and we, the observers, unaffected as we rattle along aboard the Relativity Express at speeds approaching that of light.

Meanwhile, in the real world, there was a new sound, as the vacuum was released and the brakes were applied. Almost coincident with this they passed Basford Hall. The cast-iron brake blocks snuggled into the wheels, motion converted to heat, order to disorder. Could the driver maintain control, as these unruly coaches squirmed behind him? A couple of determined timers were still measuring, but most people were content to brace themselves in their seats. George stared at the frame of the window, concentrating on the wooden beading, determined not to show his fear. How long until we hit those points? Tony Gramsci looked at George. Tony didn't know enough to realise how scared he should be. All he knew was he'd just won the sweepstake. The marshalling yards appeared, the train slowing all the time, but still going faster than George was used to.

"Fifty Five" shouted a timer, absorbed in his task.

"The points are rated at 25. And for good reason" repeated George to himself.

A noise, it wasn't the normal clatter, but something unfamiliar. George tensed. There is such a thing as being too clever for your own good. He knew they were crossing the tracks, a fact emphasised by the movement of the train to the left, shepherding them over to platform 3. *Coronation* had gracefully danced over the points. That hefty front bogie, the design borrowed by Stanier from the Great Western (who no doubt borrowed it from someone else), had stayed on the rails. The snaking coaches behind followed its lead, the only casualty was the crockery in the restaurant car, leaping off the shelves and amusing everyone, George included. They were still braking heavily as they came up to the platform, but the driver pulled up smoothly, showing his experience by releasing the brakes a little for the very last second. No sharp halt, but a gentle glide over the last couple of yards.

Tony Gramsci came into his own. He'd already got the times from Stickland and the other stop-watch amateurs and now he had started talking with the official timers, pressing them for a verdict. No mere passenger now, he was the professional communicator. The one man, amongst those present, who could take the risks they had just run and turn them into pounds, shillings and pence. They all posed for photographs, shook the drivers hand, admired the engine and patted her flanks. The official timers allowed only that they had equalled the current record – 113.5 miles per hour, but the amateurs with their stop-watches had measured 114 and the instruments on the footplate agree, allowing the LMS to claim a new world record. One hundred and fourteen miles an hour.

Reflecting on all this, scarcely twelve months later, George thinks it was a fine achievement, especially with a full rake of coaches and a limited raceway. He still allows himself a measure of pride, but the record was hardly unassailable. He looks again at this morning's headlines. Yesterday the LNER notched up 126 miles an hour, and it is their A4 loco "*Mallard*" that will enter the history books.

Rosa and the Emperor

The two spare tickets for the test match at Old Trafford had been hawked around Gathurst's for the past few days, with little interest and the bidding eventually dropped to a point that Rosa could afford them. When she told George what she had bought he was delighted. Rosa consoled herself with what a perfect girlfriend this made her, and decided to take a good book to see her through the duller parts of the day, such as any cricket that might be played.

They met without incident at Warwick Road. George had planned their journeys with great precision and abundant use of Bradshaw's. Sadly he hadn't come up with a means for them to travel together, but he had littered his latest letter to her with florid descriptions of what she might see on the journey from Liverpool Central via Ditton and Warrington to Warwick Road. It wasn't the dullest route, following the Mersey and then the ship canal before breaking for open country through Lymn and Dunham, but the scenery did little for Rosa who was simply delighted to see George again. She threw her arms around him when they met. George for his part was thrilled at the prospect of seeing first class cricket whilst in the company of a pretty and entertaining young lady and kissed her fully on the lips. They walked the short distance to the cricket ground through a lazy, lukewarm rain. The tickets Rosa had acquired were actually for rather good seats which afforded a fine view of the pitch. By a quirk of architecture they also had reasonable protection from the rain that had been lashing this particular part of Manchester for some days. The stands filled up gradually, although attendance was rather patchy, with many seemingly put off by the rain. At eleven there was no sign of the weather abating and a tinny voice said something over the address system which might have been an explanation that play would start once the rain stopped, but equally could have been somebody violating a duck with a theremin. They quickly resumed their small talk.

"Do you think we'll meet anyone famous?" enquired Rosa, feigning a naivety that was not without its charm. George still found it difficult to determine when she was pulling his leg and when she was being more earnest.

"Well, I suppose the players are famous, after a fashion."

"They're not, like, proper famous though, are they?"

"I suppose not. Who do you think of as "proper famous"?" George teased.

"An American film star! Spencer Tracey or Clark Gable!" at which Rosa made a theatrical swoon and rolled her eyes heavenward.

"I think it's unlikely they would attend an England-Australia test on a wet Sunday" George felt bad for bringing a harsh element into their fun. Rosa was irrepressible.

"I'd settle for a British film star. Or even a minor Royal. I always thought the Duke of Windsor was quite dishy." George had a picture in his mind of the former monarch in floral apron at this very moment preparing a Sunday roast for an unimpressed Wallace Simpson.

"I'm afraid you'll have to settle for present company." He said, biting his tongue at the prospect of further mischief.

"Oh well, a girl can dream" Rosa teased, in a mock New Jersey accent, learnt no doubt from countless matinees and mid-week features in the market towns of England.

"Have you ever met anyone, like, "proper famous"?" asked Rosa.

"Not really. I've met a few Bishops though my Father's trade." it was strange to talk of an Anglican priest being in "trade" but it made George more comfortable and seemed to disarm people.

"Through the church? I suppose they're important, but I wouldn't call them famous."

"I suppose not" admitted George "I've met some of the board of the LMS" he was clutching now at rather thin straws. Rosa wasn't impressed.

"I haven't really met anyone famous either" confessed Rosa, contemplating now her short but manicured finger nails for the briefest moment.

"I did once meet the King of Abyssinia" she remembered. George braced himself for a poor joke, but none was forthcoming. Somewhat reluctantly he replied

"Emperor Haile Selassie? Of Ethiopia?" certain that he was providing the punch line to the gag.

"Yes, that's him" George looked at her with incredulity

"Met him in Okehampton. In Devon. Where the cream teas come from" George tried to take this in.

"You met the Emperor Haile Selassie in a Devonshire hamlet?" he was trying to keep the incredulity out of his voice.

"Well it's more of a market town really. Old man Gathurst had a store there and sent me to sort it out. Put me up a nice hotel actually, much better than the usual guesthouses I fetch up in."

Rosa then delighted in telling her story. Her method of delivery made the Good Soldier Svejk look like a sparse and efficient reporter. She would start on the main narrative and then peel off onto a tangent, describing anything from her early life in Northumberland to the difficulty of attaching stocking to suspender in the gloom of an autumn morning.

The broad outline was that she had fetched up in Okehampton with her usual brief to sell more clothes by arranging the merchandise in an appealing manner. This was a gross simplification of her talents. After a week of her presence at a store it would have an administrative system that was simple enough for anyone to use but shrewd enough to prevent the usual frauds. The stock would be displayed to such a level of professionalism that sales leapt and even the most miserly of customer would believe they had found that elusive bargain. As the last Saturday approached there were usually a couple of members of staff, newly inspired by her, who pledged aloud to correspond and pledged to themselves to follow her example. If the world was organised according to merit, Rosa would hold the same rank as a regional manager. Gathurst himself had admitted as much to her, but the world (in any case this part of the British Empire) was not a meritocracy. The old man employed other old men as his regional managers. These managers, stuffy patricians or plump bounders almost to a man, could undo much of Rosa's good work inside of a month with a head masterly scowl in public or unsolicited and unwelcome affections in private. So Rosa made do with a wage, not a salary, a lifestyle where she was never in one place for more than a fortnight and a standard of living substantially the same as the shop girls who sought to emulate her.

Normally she would have been booked into a cheap guesthouse or bed and breakfast for the duration, but Gathurst's secretary had been unable to find a vacancy. There was an agricultural show just outside town this week, focussed mostly on swine and all things porcine. With great reluctance the secretary had to book Rosa into the one remaining room at the White Hart Hotel. It was a fairly smart coaching inn, and this was reflected in the price. When this was relayed to Rosa there was a clear undertone that such extravagance was somehow her fault. If she had stayed at a guesthouse the evening meal (tea) would have been included. At the hotel the evening meal was called dinner, was priced separately and it was made quite clear to Rosa that Gathurst's would not be picking up the bill for it. On some nights she ate from the fish and chip shop at the other end of town, on others she would make improvised meals from unbuttered bread and packets of crisps washed down with a bottle or two of fizzy pop. She had made efforts to buy a bottle of cheap wine one night but the parsimonious cow in the shop had made a fuss about whether Rosa was old enough to buy alcohol and Rosa had retreated without a fight. It was a vile and lonely existence and she longed for the next posting.

On the Thursday she awoke with the most ravenous hunger and decided to break from her normal abstinence and go down for breakfast. As she approached the dining room she could see it was very busy. Pig farmers were sat at most of the tables gorging on the products of their trade and talking loudly. Rosa's own father was a farmer but this crew were very different from old man Consett. Well healed and well fed as they appeared, she knew instinctively none of those present had seen their family farms repossessed. Neither had they had to uproot their family, zig-zagging from North East to North West and ultimately a tenancy in the South East. Their autumn and winter years would probably be spent in some leisure, whilst Rosa could see little beyond toil for her father. Resentful, but also somewhat defiant, she joined the queue to be seated.

The waitress seated those in front efficiently. Before long the tall gentlemen in front of her was dealt with and the waitress came to Rosa slightly apologetically.

"I'm sorry Miss, but we don't have any tables free at the moment, if you'd like to wait I'm sure we can seat you in half an hour." A fire burnt within Rosa. She looked from pig farmer to pig farmer, noses in the trough, each diner scarcely distinguishable from the bloated pork products they feasted on. She trembled with impotent rage, it was no use, she would have to be at the shop in three-quarters of an hour.

"Well, could you do me a bacon butty to take out?" she asked quietly, but seemingly the whole room heard her for there was an audible drop in volume and a number of faces stared at Rosa. Their countenance suggested a very grave crime had been proposed. Simultaneously the tall gentleman who had been in front of Rosa stood up.

"You would be very welcome to share my table." It was a kind and chivalrous act which might have stopped the staring faces if the gentleman proposing it hadn't been a rich dark brown in colour. Rosa smiled in gratitude at her unlikely saviour. Having worked up into a rage, she would normally take many tens of minutes to calm down. But the gentleman seemed to fill her with a beatific peace. They sat at his table and Rosa coolly gave her order to the waitress.

"Thank you" she said to her breakfast companion.

"Don't mention it. Haile Selassie, delighted to make your acquaintance….." and he volunteered his right arm across the table. Rosa was uncertain if he had said his name or something foreign which was equivalent to "nice to meet you". She met his hand with hers and chose to remove any doubt.

"Rosa Consett, it's lovely to meet you. I'm sorry I didn't catch your name" and so it was repeated.

"That sounds familiar, are you an entertainer?" And a cultured smile broke across his face to reveal a mouth of exquisite ivory. The gentleman introduced himself. Haile Selassie. Emperor of Ethiopia, now living in exile as Italian Fascists strutted across his homeland. But of course he explained it so much better. He was seemingly without hatred, only concern for his people. And even as he explained all this he was concerned also for Rosa, that she should get her breakfast without excessive haste. But also that he shouldn't detain her too long and make her late for work.

Rosa ate her breakfast and enjoyed the company of the Emperor, as she was now mentally referring to him. As she finished she made her excuses and rose to leave. The Emperor then asked her to join him for dinner. Without a thought she accepted. It was only on the walk to work she was troubled by misgivings. There was of course the indisputable fact of his colour. Rosa had no doubt that dining with a black man, however exalted his station would arose the permanent wrath of her father, if he ever found out. Well that, if anything, was one good reason to *keep* the date. Then there was the cost of dinner. In England only the worst kind of cad would expect a lady to pay for her dinner, but Rosa had a habit of finding the worst kind of cad. And who was to say that it was a universal convention. After all there was the phrase "Going Dutch" which she understood to mean they split the bill equally. If this happened in Amsterdam why not in Addis Ababa? And then there was her final doubt. Supposing he wasn't really who he said he was? What if he was a procurer of young women? That he slipped something into her drink tonight, and tomorrow she woke up bound in the hold of a ship destined for the harems of Arabia. She kept coming back to this one, with images in her mind of insatiable olive-skinned sheiks and a certain obsession on her part as to what form the skimpy clothing of the harem-girl may take. She thought red and orange would go best with her hair and skin tone.

At this stage George felt he had waited long enough for the punch line and pressed her to deliver it.

"No really, that's what I thought!" implored Rosa with an unforced smile upon her face. "I felt really bad even thinking that about him. After how kind he had been at breakfast. And of course I know now he really was genuine, but a girl can't be too careful these days." George let it go and allowed the fact that it was unlikely the white slave trade had yet extended its reach into rural Devon. Rosa resumed her story.

She was kept busy at work moving stock around and arranging displays. She scarcely got a chance to sit down, with the result that her feet ached by the afternoon. Rosa got back to the hotel at just after six and soaked in a bath drawn exclusively from the hot tap. She felt drowsy as she got out but prepared herself with enthusiasm. She was rather looking forward to a posh meal and had put her doubts about the Emperor to the back of her mind.

He met her in reception as arranged and they walked through into the restaurant. What the hotel staff thought is not recorded but they were a picture of hospitality to the pair. An easy dialog followed for the whole night. He spoke of his wife and family. Rosa told him about her own family and circumstances. She asked him about his country, partly from a sense of courtesy, partly from a curiosity she had not previously known she possessed. He spoke of the high plains on which the air was thin and every breath was hard won, of the depths of the Afar valley where saline lakes sat 500 feet below sea level. His pride in his countrymen and their sense of history, of independence and of fair play shone through his testimony.

Rosa learnt how Ethiopia was mentioned in the holy books of Jews, Christians and Muslims and had received each with hospitality. He recalled with pride how his, the only independent African nation, had been a founder member of the League of Nations, although he did not dwell on how badly that organisation had let him down. At Rosa's request he did elaborate on the Italian invasion, though it clearly upset him. She recalled the headlines, such as had been published in the Beaverbook and Rothermere Press. She thought she remembered tales of poison gas, although she couldn't be sure and she would rather not ask.

What surprised her was that he couldn't find anger for an individual Italian soldier. His anger was limited to the false prophets who had led these boys astray. For them his language was biblical in its ferocity and he apologised as he reined in his ire. Rosa, hitherto an apolitical animal felt compelled to do something to help this man and his country. As was her style she asked openly what she might do. He considered his reply for some time, but rather than encourage her to contribute to the Red Cross or work for the overthrow of fascism he said simply:

"Love with all your heart, and with all your soul, and with all your strength, and with all your mind; and love your neighbour as yourself."

It seemed familiar to Rosa but she fancied she had never heard anything more beautiful in her life and only through a supreme effort of will did she not cry. Her bottom lip trembled and the Emperor reached across to steady her hand. Sometime later they bid farewell as they had met, at the entrance to the dining room door. The Emperor was leaving for Bath in the morning whilst Rosa would be leaving for her next store on Saturday afternoon.

George realised now that there would be no punch line, that his Rosa had depths he had yet to fully appreciate. He thought back to those events in winter 'thirty-five and spring 'thirty-six. Would he have fought alongside the Ethiopians if his government had appealed for him to do so? He knew he would have dodged it if there was any lawful way to avoid it. As it was, his government had dodged the issue for him. England might be an imperfect and flawed democracy but the National Government truly represented the will of the people. And its people blandly tolerated them for it.

Reading Room 5

Access to Reading Room 5 was not granted to everyone, or so they had told Jacob on arrival. His fellow readers are not inclined to friendliness, so it is impossible to reach any definite answer. In the semi-darkness he sits, wrestling with his discoveries, for they are manifold. Assays have given some insight but confirm also that the chemical composition remains constant with time. Concluding, reasonably enough that this rules out a chemical reaction, Jacob has allowed his mind to wander. He speculates whether such daydreams are the mark of a great mind or an average one. He has yet to draw a conclusion.

Today he is reading up on phase changes, latent heat, and other physical phenomena that frustrate common sense. In Jacob's mind is the possibility his South African ore imposes a different structure upon the water in which it is dissolved. For he recalls from his education what a curious individual water is. A rebel amongst the commonly occurring compounds, neither melting nor evaporating in quite the way we would predict. And capable of carrying prodigious quantities of heat. As a policeman might round up the usual suspects, it is entirely understandable that Jacob should turn his attention to the medium, not the additive.

So, he asks of himself, is there a different way of ordering things? Isn't that the phrase of the moment? His mind makes another giant leap, from the physical sciences to the social. Those efficient foreign ideas that have so galvanised Germany, Italy and Russia. Never mind the human souls that stand in the way. Look at the fantastic achievements, the white concrete and steel, the order of it all. Even Jacob, who might have more to lose than most where such a millennial event to happen here, is nonetheless impressed by the sheer *progress*. So today it is structure we are looking into, to the bonds and the energies hidden in every glass of water. And why not? Because investigation has to start somewhere, does it not?

Jacob looks up from his studies. Tries to get his bearings and recall where the toilets are, to weigh up his fellow researchers without being observed doing so. They are a curious mix, these readers, students, academics, the plain curious or the woefully underemployed.

He trusts none of them, just as they don't trust him. Oh, he could leave his wallet upon the table with absolute certainty that it would be unmolested. But his notebook accompanies him to the lavatory. He stops, shocked at his own transformation. Yesterday he caught himself staring at a sharply dressed chap who happened to have been in the previous week. Jacob had found himself wondering what an employee of Deutsche Reichsbahn might look like. When did knowledge become something to hoard jealously, rather than share freely? Not for the first time he wonders at the ambivalent honour his discoveries may have conferred upon him.

Momenta

Philipa walked through to the kitchen and placed the kettle on the stove. She became aware of the cool tiled floor on her bare feet. She pulled the night gown a little tighter around herself, a five foot six hourglass amongst the Lilliput kitchen utensils. She rummaged through the cupboards, searching for a seldom used pack of aspirins. Once located, she drank them down with a glass of water and returned upstairs. In the bedroom last night's companion was still asleep, snoozing face down, tousled blond curls resting on the pillows, flawless back exposed down to a neat, plump rear. "We had some jolly japes" Philipa smiled to herself "even though we will both be embarrassed this morning." She carefully retrieved the lipstick-marked wineglasses and tiptoed down stairs.

As the kettle showed no immediate signs of boiling she padded through to the hall and collected the Sunday paper. There had been a time when she took two, three even four papers of a Sunday, but Philipa was glad she now took only one. It was a promising indication of a life well lived. A cigarette was lit and the headlines were scanned. There was no substantive news, instead just a reworking of the events of the past few months. There was a little human interest piece about an act of minor heroism. There was also a large headline proclaiming something extravagant, which on inspection was no more than an aspiration from an anonymous "well-placed source".

One article caught Philipa's eye. It was on the European situation, and Philipa had to admire it, if only for the creativity of its author. Here was outlined a fine exposition of collective security. The author imagined a quartet of Britain, France, Russia and the United States hammering out a joint declaration to contain Hitler and Mussolini. The author had done his homework, for there were supportive quotes from all quarters. The real substance rested with whether the speakers would ever be bold enough to have their remarks attributed to them, and whether they could exert power behind their respective thrones. The article ended with some conjuring around the words "inertia" and "momentum". It ignited a cautious optimism in Philipa and, free to dream of other matters, she regarded herself in the full length mirror on the opposite wall.

"I might have made a fine model for Rossetti or Holman Hunt" she thought, sitting herself on the sofa, unashamed of the simple harmonic motion this set off about her body.

"It is true, you could be Prosperpine or Pandora" answered someone beyond the threshold of human hearing. It was Porlock, one of two identical black cats of the Arden residence, stalking towards the sofa to continue her observations.

"What a choice? As Prosperpine I would usher in the seasons, year in year out, whilst as Pandora I would, by my curiosity, unleash all hell on earth."

"So, Pandora it is then?"

"You know me too well. Defying the gods and shaping my own destiny, whatever the consequences – that's just my cup tea. Remember, though, that once all evil had escaped Pandora was left with hope at the bottom of her box."

"Well we have found your character, we just need an artist."

"In my youth I was asked by an artist friend to pose unclothed. How shocked and thrilled I was! I declined, of course. But now I am no longer young. Perhaps I may yet fulfil that queer ambition?" reflected Philipa.

"Last night you were young again."

"True. And it is with a certain satisfaction I see middle age accumulating chiefly upon my hips and my bust and continue to receive unsolicited glances from all ages"

"The Merry Widow."

"Hah! Not quite, for I will never be rid of my sorrows. I am, more accurately, a highly respectable wife, for I do nothing that would have shocked Alfred." She cast her gaze back at the papers.

"Dear Alfred what might you have made of all this? A passionate conversation at the dinner table I am sure. And a passionate night we would have too. You know, my love don't you? You know that I think only of you as the crescendo arrives? And that the tears I oft times weep in the golden afterwards are yours?"

Prufrock, the other cat joined them, the two cats conducting a wary circling routine before settling in front of the unlit hearth and becoming indistinguishable from each other.

"I should never have got two identical cats."

"No two cats are identical, you should know that Philipa. But I understand you are talking of our outward appearance?"

"Indeed."

"Then the greater censure I would save for your choice of names."

"Oh? I think they suit you."

"As a regular interruption to your muse, I plead guilty, but why name my sister Prufrock? You should know we cats have no appreciation for language, only tone. It's terribly confusing."

"Pity me, then, for having to shout the two names as dusk approaches."

"Philipa, as a human you will always enjoy feline pity."

"Pity me also for my advancing age, sat talking only to my cats. I am become cliché."

"Our pity is bottomless, of course. As is our contempt." and with that Porlock licked her front paws.

"Prufrock?" Philipa asked in search of support. The other cat wanted to help, if only to spite her sister. But all she gave away was a single blink of her yellow eyes.

"Inertia" thought Philipa

"That tendency for things to remain stationary, to resist movement."

"Oh you are awake! Thank you sweetie, yes that makes sense."

"Endowed on an object by virtue of its mass."

"Mass? You mean its bulk? How big it is?"

"No, that is not quite what I meant. Weight if you would prefer, though even that is slightly inaccurate"

"So my weight endows inertia? That explains a lot" thought Philipa.

"We are talking physics here, not metaphysics. Your own inertia has more to do with the two bottles of Cote de Rhone from last night and a certain laziness because you think the Sabbath is an excuse for indolence."

"One can grow tired of pets, you know? Every man should eat and drink, and enjoy the good of all his labour, it is the gift of God."

"Don't quote the King James Version at me, young lady. One can grow tired of owners too."

"Touché."

"Miaow."

A momentary silence.

"You know, Prufrock, On days like this I might be happy?"

"You have every reason to be, given the bohemian company you are keeping."

"I have no regrets" said Philipa.

"And no surprises" riposted Prufrock.

"And my work has gained such momentum."

"Ah the M word. Would you care for a definition?"

"If it will keep you out of mischief, yes."

"Momentum. A product of the mass and the velocity of an object in motion."

"Velocity? Another word for speed?"

"The speed in a particular direction, yes. Stick with velocity, my dear, you know where you are with velocity."

"So the more I weigh, the greater my momentum?"

"All other things being equal, yes."

"I think I understand."

"I have my doubts."

"So inertia is just a tendency, whilst momentum is a measurable property?"

"By Jove, I think she's got! Though don't be so dismissive. Personally I find inertia to be the more interesting concept. It prompts so many more questions."

"Just like my Night Watchman. So many stories, such fertile ground. Its like an express train steaming now down the mainline, the fireman throwing coal into the grate, the driver opening the regulator to its fullest, pulling all along behind in the slipstream of history."

"Ah, the romance of the steam train! Best enjoyed by the middle class at rest, and always at some remove from the sweaty toil of the workers. Still there may be more than a grain of truth in what you say. But doesn't it bother you? Doing history on the strength of hearsay?"

"I've occasionally woken in the early hours and fretted I've taken a wrong turning, but I know I've hit on something, Prufrock, mark my words."

"Remember when you knitted that jumper for the Abyssinia Appeal?"

"Oh dear, it became a frightful mess, didn't it?"

"It did, and all because you failed to start with a nice firm knot. There's a lesson there."

“Hmm” said Philipa.
“Miaow” said Prufrock.
“Time for toast and tea” said Philipa.
“…and a time to weep, and a time to laugh.”
“A time to mourn, and a time to dance.”

If I had a million dollars

George cast an avaricious glance at the retreating motor car. An MG TA, ebony black and with the roof down. In the driver's seat sat an affluent looking young man – probably old money judging by the cut of the jacket. In the passenger seat sat an attractive specimen, probably a little too young for the driver, but money can mask many a flaw, including the flaw of getting old. Blonde, why were they always blonde? She wasn't George's cup of tea – a little too skinny and doubtless very high maintenance. Just like the MG. It was the car that was the cause of his avarice. He'd loved cars since he was a boy, but this new MG, it was a real smasher. He allowed a brief daydream of what owning such a car might mean. Well, for one thing there'd be no more trips on smoky railways and no more walks of a mile or two at his destination. He'd have the run of the road, and park right outside at journeys end. He'd need petrol, and tyres, and he'd have to maintain it. But he was an engineer – it couldn't be too difficult. And anyway, working on an engine would be like a hobby – a welcome relief from the Brontosauruses of the LMS. Oh, to own that MG. It was on his list – "Things to do by 'forty-two". By his latest reckoning he would be able to get a mortgage on a house next year – maybe one of the new bay-fronted semis in the better part of town. He almost had the deposit. Things would be tight at first, but if he started saving again he should be able to have the MG, on the never-never, by late 'forty-one. He could just picture himself and Rosa, getting out of the MG, bathed in afternoon sunlight, his arm casually draping itself around her waist. That was worth fighting for, and b------- to Hitler, or Chamberlain.

It had been one of those days where rather too many choices present themselves. In theory, at least, you could take yourself to the coast, and watch as the waves lap against our island. You could even roll your trousers up and feel the water, cold despite the sunshine, washing gritty sand between your toes. Or you could venture into the hills, and walk hard until each breath is like fire, drawn directly through the mouth into hungry lungs, whilst your heart announces itself with every beat. Or perhaps you could fetch up lazily in one of the spa towns, taking tea and cake in a genteel little cafe and pottering in stores that languish half a century or more in the past. There are plenty of alternatives to a person with even a modest amount of money. Even without the MG, from Crewe station you could be at any of those destinations in little more than an hour.

George however had failed to come to any conclusion. He wandered instead into Queens Park through the gates on Victoria Avenue. The park was a welcome relief from the redbrick and coal smoke that infused much of the rest of the town. Having been raised in the countryside George felt a degree of peace here, amongst trees and lakes. It wasn't anything he could put his finger on, just an aspect of life that was otherwise absent from his normal urban existence. Today was the penultimate Sunday in August. Rosa was travelling to Maidstone for the usual two week tour of duty. Mrs Minshull was performing a spring clean, despite the house already being aseptic. George had therefore been shooed out after breakfast and given to understand that a return before tea time may well lead to permanent eviction. He had read the Sunday papers for most of the morning and then took lunch at one of Crewe's better public houses, but now it was afternoon and the number of activities to keep one occupied was dwindling. With a feeling of indulging a childish habit George had bought a cheap loaf from a corner shop and was on his way to the duck pond. He breathed the wet, loamy odour of the park into his chest with a feeling of drawing sustenance from it. A spell of rain just before noon had encouraged the slugs to come out and they were currently making their multi-hued way slowly across the path. Having never been a gardener, George had a tolerant attitude to their presence. They were as much a part of the park as the ducks or the rhododendrons. The duck pond itself was quiet. The rain, having encouraged the slugs, had also cleared most of the people. George was glad. Feeding the ducks ought to be a lonely pursuit. A spot of solitude would help him resolve things.

There is a certain art to feeding the ducks. A small child will rip large hunks off the bread, throwing them wildly and giggling in delight as they land like naval ordinance amongst this latter-day re-enactment of the Battle of Jutland. Laughter quickly turns to tears, however, as they exhaust the supply. A more experienced duck feeder will instead pinch modest pieces of bread off and distribute it widely throughout the flotilla. This will have the effect of providing for most of the brood, whilst the soft ripples also encourage the more shy specimens into the open. When one feeds the ducks in this way it is not unknown for mother duck and her ducklings to eventually join the fray. There is of course the problem of larger wild fowl. Geese and Swans are the principal interlopers. The vicious nature of Swans is widely documented, but Canada Geese also show a particular greed, often attacking the smaller birds or each other. In such circumstances the best advice is to stop feeding. Should they come hissing out of the water at you, having identified you as the food source, an umbrella flapped open and closed will convince them to back down. Recalling all of this, George resolved that he would one day commit his knowledge to a pamphlet or short book. It would likely be one of those vanity projects, put out only by virtue of the author paying for publishing himself. The sort of thing that remainders after fifty three copies, the unsold print run languishing in dusty second hand book shops. Perhaps he would buy the house and the MG first.

By some autonomic response George had already begun feeding the ducks. By turns his thoughts wandered off onto other matters. Mrs Arden. The very fact he still thought of her as Mrs Arden, and not Philipa, said everything. It defined her as part of a couple, even with the other half killed on a foreign field some twenty years ago. Was she enigmatic? If you insist on such language, yes. She was unattainable, that was for certain. What had first attracted George? There were the physical charms, but that was rather obvious. What had sustained his interest? The easy manner and the sure touch with the world, true. But, what had really attracted him was the co-conspirator, me-and-you-against-them-all attitude, which it turned out was something she could turn on for any man, Maxwell, Werner, doubtless her patron (whoever and whatever he might be) and maybe even Inspector Kaye. It certainly didn't confer any special intimacy or privilege. It was a coin of low value, however striking its appearance. With all this in mind George had ceased to reply to her letters. Indeed he hadn't written since the Doncaster visit. Not since Rosa. It was a rude thing to do, for Philipa had been kind enough to him, but he needed the separation. He also reasoned, correctly, that his lack of correspondence would not represent a loss, grievous or otherwise, to the pattern of her days. He resolved now that he should nonetheless underline this, and mentally composed a letter of farewell:

Dear Mrs Arden,

I have enjoyed our acquaintance but I have recently met a young lady who holds a particular affection in my heart and I feel it would be inappropriate for the two of us to continue corresponding. This may seem somewhat old fashioned, or parochial, but I know that you will respect my beliefs.

Yours Sincerely,

George Bradfield.

He reached into his paper bag, but the bread was now exhausted. Emptying the crumbs onto the surface of the pond he gazed into the middle distance, eyes focussed vaguely on the distant swans. He tried to recall past triumphs, past failures, insults accepted, joys debased, daring his demons to make an appearance. But just like the rest of the town, the demons had been put off by the rain and were instead sleeping off their Sunday roast in front of the radio.

And so that left Rosa. Oh dear, sweet Rosa. He struggled to fashion the words to describe his feelings for her. The way she took delight in the littlest of life's pleasures. Fizzy pop and gentle curves. That was what had first attracted him. But she was a deeper, more thoughtful person than all that. She professed no great knowledge of the world, and was self-deprecating when it came to her grasp of current affairs – "I'm a bit thick, really" she would say. But break any argument down into first principles and she could grasp it instantly, and could then voice an enlightened opinion. George turned away from the duck pond, heading back towards the town. He didn't dare to make plans with Rosa, not yet. Bitter past experience had unmasked the most valiant of his plans as nothing more than dust that built on dust. "And though I speak with the tongues of men and of angels…" but he stopped that thought before it bloomed. He had hope. That would have to do, at least for now. He slowed as he passed the pavilion. Some patient soul was listening to the cricket on the radio. Hutton had racked up close to 300 runs. The commentator was speculating lazily on the English strategy. Would one of the lower-order batsmen be brought on as a night watchman? Oh sweet conspiracy. George chuckled to himself as he wandered home.

Cat and Mouse

Stickland passed the telephone receiver across to George, the braided wire pulling dangerously taut, only the immense weight of the base preventing the whole phone from yo-yoing across the desk. Stickland returned to his work, conscious of the remaining labours of this afternoon but mind drifting also to the impending release of evening

George announced himself into the mouthpiece with a voice tired after the day at work. It was nearly time to go home and he wasn't prepared for distractions, whether they came from Mr Stanier, Sir Josiah Stamp or the Duchess of Buccleuch.

"Good evening George" purred the voice on the other end of the line.

"Mrs Arden" he replied frostily.

"I'm in town for the next couple of hours, would you care to meet me?"

George was uncertain what to say. He was never happy delivering unwelcome news, but prided himself that he wouldn't tiptoe around it.

"I'm not sure that's a good idea. Did you get my letter?"

"Yes I did, thank you very much. It certainly put me in my place. However I need your help. Would you be able to help a damsel in distress?" With that she let out a coquettish giggle.

"Philipa...." He started to say something, but words wouldn't come to him. He wanted to say that he was trying to get on with his own life, to build something with Rosa. But all the while he felt the ghost of Alfred Arden staring at him, looking on disappointedly, brooding how he had given his life for George's future and now George couldn't even spare an hour to look after his widow. George was reluctantly struck by a vision of Philipa as some latter-day Lady Hamilton.

"You must do whatever you think is right, of course" answered Philipa sadly. "I'll be in the buffet on platform 4 for the next hour".

George was gripped by a desire to help as much as he could, but he would play an absolutely straight bat. He would make it clear they couldn't meet again. He would do the right thing this time and tell Inspector Kaye. He pulled the number for the Inspector out of his wallet, dialled and asked to be put through. He was conscious of his own heartbeat as he waited to be answered. At the fourth ring George was concerned. By the sixth he knew instinctively the phone at the other end was announcing itself to an empty office. It was almost half past five, but surely they must have someone he could speak to? He put the phone down and rang again, this time asking for anyone in Inspector Kaye's department.

"You'll be lucky" replied a surly male voice, presumably the security guard or doorman, manning the phones now that the secretaries had left for the evening. "This isn't exactly your local police station, sunshine. If it's such an emergency why don't you ring 999?" And with that helpful advice the phone went dead. If there was ever another war, George hoped it started in business hours.

He was now in a fresh quandary and resorted to asking for Stickland's opinion, for what it was worth. Once the licentious comments about George's prospects with Philipa's virtue were dispensed with the Mathematician adopted an unexpectedly avuncular tone.

"It is the finest thing a man can do: to betray his country for his friend." George looked at him in confusion. The man was serious.

"You are a person of impeccable principles, George, correct in your behaviour and an inspiration to others of more venial leanings." Stickland continued, pointing at himself.

"I cannot in good faith advise you, dear boy, because I do not aspire to the lofty heights of your morality. I am one of the damned." Stickland paused and George looked at him blankly. This wasn't helping particularly.

"Of course, you must do whatever you think is right" concluded Stickland, as if repeating a long remembered mantra. George looked at him, a ripple of electricity running down his spine and back again. Wasn't that the exact phrase Philipa had used? Was there the faintest glint of a smile on that cultured, dead-pan face?

"Thank you" replied George.

"I'll walk with you to the station" suggested Stickland.

It was a most splendid evening. The day had been rather hot, and their office had warmed to an unpleasant temperature, but outside there was a gentle breeze and George fancied he caught the smell of tree blossom. The light had that warm quality that a setting sun lends to a landscape.

"I always imagined the Garden of Gethsemane would be like this" muttered Stickland.

"What's that?" asked George, looking up at him.

"Oh, don't pay me any attention, just trying to relieve a bad case of writers block." Rather embarrassed, Stickland scratched the bridge of his nose with the back of his forefinger, another thought having occurred to him. "Listen, old man, I think I might be able to help you." George looked at him hopefully. "Just don't ask too many questions" the Mathematician added cryptically. They had reached the railway station now and both men bought a platform ticket. They bid each other good bye and good luck. George paused for a moment before making for platform 4 whilst Stickland walked briskly towards platform 5. Platforms 4 and 5 were separated by an expanse of four separate lines. As George arrived on platform 4 he heard a commotion from across the lines. A brawl had erupted on platform 5 which already involved a number of people and seemed to be escalating in intensity. The railway police were sprinting now into the fray, whistles blowing in an attempt to restore order. George slipped into the buffet on platform 4 unobserved. He found her easily enough at a corner table. She smiled warmly.

"I knew you would come."

"Would you mind telling me what the hell I am getting myself into?" asked George.

"All in good time, we have more than an hour before my train comes. Tea?" and without answer she poured him a cup from the small pot on the table.

"Thank you" he answered from years of programming.

"You are aware of my interest in the Night Watchman?"

"Yes" George was about ready to leave. He should have known it would involve that old chestnut. This was going to take some explaining to the Inspector in the morning.

"Well for some time I've been aware of Inspector Kaye's interest too. You might say we've played a little game of cat-and-mouse, neither of us being too willing to give our hand away to the other."

"I'm well aware of the games the two of you have been playing. It's lead to some very unpleasant threats to me and those I … hold dear."

"Careful George, you nearly used the L-word" teased Philipa.

"Well damn you then, yes, those I love"

"How is your little shop girl?"

"That was rather cheap. We can't all be history professors." Philipa looked away, not exactly embarrassed, but aware that she hadn't acquitted herself very well.

"Are you still ready to sell your soul for domestic tranquillity?" She continued.

"I thought you wanted my help?"

"I do. But I'm curious. I thought you had fallen for me." A wan smile was across her face, she lit a cigarette, Players No. 6.

"Maybe there was a time. But I came to realise you will forever be Mrs Arden."

"I admire your insight. Other men have turned themselves into silly, love-sick puppies and still not come to terms with that essential truth." She took a long draw on the cigarette, the end burning a vibrant orange, and exhaled gently into empty space.

"I fell for you, in my own way" she admitted, holding the cigarette hand now close to her face, forearm and elbow defensive across her chest. She was embarrassed at having made this admission and looked off into infinity. "I doubt we would have lasted though." She wore a brief, foolish smile.

"I know" answered George.

"Do you really love this Rosa?"

"Yes. Yes I do."

"A cynic might conclude it's all a bit soon after your infatuation with me?"

"Well, let them conclude what they like. I know what I believe." George felt filled with a mighty conviction that this was true. He loved Rosa. In that moment came the revelation that it wasn't false hope or a clutching at straws. It certainly wasn't second-best. It was a feeling deep within his core.

"We should all meet up one day. When all this is over" suggested Philipa. George was not enthusiastic at this prospect. They both took a draft of tea.

"I wish you well."

"Thank you" answered George rather stiffly, prepared for another barbed comment.

"Would you mind telling me why you dragged me here?"

"Patience, Mr Bradfield, patience" but she also had an eye on the clock, so began to explain.

"Well, I have had a grand old year so far, chasing around after this Night Watchman. It really has been a splendid way to spend the spring and summer. I've fetched up in Berwick and Penzance, Canterbury and Carlisle and all points in between. I've met miners, industrial chemists, engineers, aircraft technicians and all manner of other trades. I've collected some remarkable histories and fables and all I have to do is fashion them into a credible treatise for my patron."

"How many of these other poor souls have you seduced?"

"My word! Who's being cheap now, George?"

"You have my apologies for any offence caused." They looked at one another with steely, passionless faces and then both laughed because neither could maintain the illusion.

"As I said, I have thoroughly enjoyed myself. But it became apparent that I had aroused the interest of a certain Inspector Kaye. Now, I was curious. Why would a shadowy copper from the Metropolitan police be interested in me and the Night Watchman? So I have spent the past couple of months playing a little game with him, seeing how far I could push him, trying to tease out his motives".

"And what have you discovered?"

"Absolutely nothing."

"Well congratulations, you are the world's worst conspirator" jibed George.

"Not quite, my dear George." Her cigarette had burnt down to her fingers and she tapped out another one and lit it. George didn't remember her as a chain smoker from their previous encounters. Did this hint at some inner turmoil? Or was he drawing wild conclusions? Welcome to the world of conspiracies, real and imagined.

"Our little game is very simple, consisting of just two possible moves in any one round. I can either run, or I can surrender to the Inspector. He can either have me trailed, or he can apprehend me. That is it. Everything else is just a subtle variant. We have played a few rounds and it has, as I say, been fun."

"That's not quite the whole story, because the pair of you have dragged innocents into this. Such as me. And Rosa."

"Innocents! Oh God bless your little Anglican heart. I suppose you are right. You are so innocent of this world, and you expect so little from it! But no, George, that is the whole story. You have been inconvenienced and nothing more. I am sorry for that, really I am, but it was unavoidable."

"And yet, Philipa, you need my help?"

"Yes I do. The game is stuck. We both know how the other will react. Any further running on my part will not yield more information. Equally, however, it is not in my interest to surrender, for that would indicate guilt on my part."

"And for the Inspector, further trailing of you will not reveal any new information?"

"Exactly"

"And if he apprehended you ... actually why doesn't he just have you arrested?"

"Friends in high places, dear George."

"Oh?"

"Widow of a war hero, working for a well-respected Liberal politician, arrested for a bit of research into some harmless folklore. The papers would have a field day. He would need to have very good evidence, and he has next to nothing." Philipa smiled smugly. George noticed that Philipa had been drawing out a little square on her newspaper, with the options written down. Every game resulted in both players selecting "Run" and "Trail". George was fascinated. It looked like a mathematics puzzle.

"So what's the plan? And how do I feature in it?"

"I want you to betray me." George felt a shiver. He would have been less shocked if she had suggested they make love on the table. Betrayal was not a word used lightly in the Bradfield household.

"I want you to call the good Inspector tomorrow morning and report our meeting. Don't miss a detail, even down to the gamesmanship and this piece of paper. I want the Inspector to have me arrested." She drew some additional jottings demonstrating how this slewed the game.

"I might not be following this very well, but it seems to me that betrayal doesn't guarantee that you will be arrested."

"No, but it changes the values. It introduces an uncertainty. The game is, you might say, indeterminate."

"Might I also observe that you could be in for a rough ride if you do force the Inspectors hand and get arrested."

"It's just a game George. I'm hardly going to be hauled off to Siberia, or even Holloway. At the worst I'll have a few days of unpleasantness in the cells of the Met. I've probably slept in more lousy hostels travelling in the Near East."

"I don't like the idea of this. I don't betray my friends, and I still count you as a friend regardless of everything."

"Oh George! You need to stop being quite so prim. It'll be a lark. As an innocent accused of a crime I haven't committed I'll be able to tease out the Inspector's interest in all this." George remained sceptical. He was unconvinced the game really did breakdown into these simple binary choices. It occurred to him that she had become rather attracted to the danger itself. But then she wasn't really proposing anything he hadn't intended to do already. They argued for some minutes, neither of them saying anything original.

"Why would you put yourself in this position? Surely you could just complete your book with what you have learnt so far?"

"I hope you won't be offended, but do you really understand History as an academic discipline?"

"I think so. It's about what happened in the past isn't it?"

"It's all about an objective investigation into cause and effect. As a historian I strive to really understand why things happened. It's not just about recording what happened."

"I still don't understand why you have to take such risks?"

"I suppose it is in my nature. I could never be satisfied with a bland compromise." She shrugged.

"If you are certain this is what you want I'll do it, but only on two conditions."

"And what would they be?"

"Well firstly, that you send me a single letter when it is all over, from wherever you are, telling me what the outcome was. I wouldn't be able to live with myself if I didn't know what had become of you."

"You old softy! I knew you still cared" said Philipa, turning on her old charm. But George was quick to dispel any misunderstanding.

"And secondly, that you respect the position I outlined in my last letter. I cannot continue to see you and conduct a relationship with Rosa."

"I understand. And I really do wish you well."

The next day at work George was scribbling his thoughts onto a sheet of paper, trying to steel himself to his awful duty. It was almost ten before Stickland made an appearance. George looked up. He looked much the same as always, the same immaculate appearance, the same flawless, upper-middle class face. It was only as he went to remove the cover from his typewriter that George noticed his hands. The knuckles of each hand were an angry, inflamed red colour and the skin was split in several places. He moved his hands with a deliberate slowness, quickly abandoning any effort to uncover the typewriter.

"You wouldn't have a soft pencil, by any chance?" He asked George.

"Would a 2B do?"

"Just the ticket" he said with a wince. George carried it over to him.

George nodded silently towards Stickland's knuckles.

"You should have seen my opponent" he answered with a dangerous smile. George did not want to contemplate the damage those mighty hands had wrought.

"Don't feel too bad, old man, the truly innocent were spared. I consider my actions as having merely brought forward an inevitable piece of aggravation, and inflicted the damage only upon the guilty." George was nonetheless unsettled at such summary justice. He fetched a cup of tea for his colleague and acquainted him with Philipa's request.

"So you are in the happy position of having to betray neither friend nor country. You do indeed lead a charmed life, Mr Bradfield." And, with a friendly smile, he passed George the telephone and had him call the Inspector.

Compromising

It was a dull, grey Sunday in September. The day was already fading into afternoon when Rosa first arrived at the guesthouse. Now she had just finished unpacking her clothes and sat on the bed looking out of the window. The guesthouse was opposite a T-junction and Rosa's room was to the front, with the result that the window gave a fine view down the street. It wasn't a busy road, the traffic being mostly bicycles and pedestrians, with the occasional horse. Some children were playing with a ball in the middle of the street. Once in a while a car would drive slowly along the street, the driver simultaneously trying to avoid the aforementioned hazards whilst also playing the choke in and out to avoid stalling the car at the slow speed that was necessary.

The Gathurst machinery had dispatched Rosa to Northampton for the next fortnight. She hadn't previously been to Northampton and tried to muster some enthusiasm for exploring. She knew in advance what limited pleasures any English town would hold. There would be a cinema or two, and maybe a down-at-heel music hall or theatre. There would be pubs and bars from which she wasn't in theory excluded, but where her presence, unaccompanied, would make her the target of speculation or unwelcome attention. There would likely be libraries and perhaps a gallery or museum which would close just as she herself finished work. To entertain oneself for a week in a strange town, on limited means, was not easy, but Rosa made an effort. The Cinema would probably be good for one night. She was also known to attend public meetings in anything from a church hall to a social club. In the past few years she had heard from the Young Farmers, the League of Nations, the Towns Women's Guild, the Peace Pledge Union, the Left Book Club, the Women's Institute, Moral Rearmament and a confident, handsome young man with a big nose who had something to do with the Sommelier's Guild. She didn't take all of it in, and occasionally read a book discretely at the back of the hall, but it felt more like real life than sitting in the parlour of the guesthouse, or the parlour of the Consett family home for that matter.

Some minutes later, still sat on her bed, Rosa was summoned down for tea. The landlady had contrived to make a hearty roast dinner, but had also contrived to do it for as little money as possible. Rosa examined her plate of food. It probably contained all the necessary nutrition but the lavish portions of vegetables only served to make the meat look miserly.

Rosa started eating with her mind on other things. She thought of George, as she had found herself doing rather often in the past few weeks. In the first weeks of their meeting Rosa had been determined not to invest too much hope in the relationship. Her past experience had taught her that the initial bloom usually wilted into recrimination and disappointment. As their days together proceeded without this disappointment, she still didn't dare to hope for fear of offending God, or fate, or whoever, by being too presumptuous.
It was now almost three months since they first met, and there was still a sparkle of magic every time she thought of George. But he also had habits that annoyed her. She wished he was more willing to talk about his feelings, about his fears, and less willing to rant about the world around him. A couple of weeks ago they had got to talking, in the most general terms, about war. George had said he would rather not fight and Rosa had pushed him as to why not. Would he be a conscientious objector? Rosa was herself ambivalent on this. She didn't like the idea of George down a coal mine and she certainly didn't see him as a farm hand. It became clear his desire to avoid fighting was not from cowardice, but nor was it from principle. He just didn't want to. It wasn't how he planned to spend his time. Rosa found the attitude rather quaint but despaired whether it could ever be put into practice. George for his part shrugged, smiled, threw his arms around her and kissed her on the nose.

She looked back at her roast dinner. She conceded to herself that the carrots were nice and crisp. The cabbage complimented the boiled potato perfectly and the stuffing was splendid.

Peace for our time

Rosa was kept particularly busy in Northampton. The papers were full of speculation as to whether Czechoslovakia would cede Sudetenland. This technicality rather went over most people's heads but the prospect of war suddenly seemed more immediate to everyone. The good people of Northampton had therefore mobilized and occupied Gathurst's in a series of dawn-to-dusk manoeuvres designed to furnish themselves with a new suit or a raincoat. The in-store hire-purchase scheme was particularly popular, with more than one customer explaining they were intending to take out huge loans on the certain expectation of civilisation itself being destroyed in the coming weeks. Rosa, who was slightly more optimistic as to the survival of civilisation, privately shuddered at the weekly payments on the form she filled out for them.

She had found herself pulled in as an extra pair of hands to serve the customers and had no time during the normal working day to sort out the administration or to re-arrange the merchandise. She found herself working into the evenings and was denied the pleasures of the Odeon as well as having to miss a lecture with the cryptic title "How to avoid getting eaten by a crocodile". The pace was solid for nearly two weeks, and Rosa felt tired beyond belief. She awoke every morning with a vague doubt that she had left something undone from the previous day. Letters from George sustained her, but she scarcely had the time to read them and replies were hastily scribbled whilst eating her lunch.

The news was something she heard other people discuss. In any event she had never been terribly interested in current affairs, and the present crisis didn't interest her particularly. The papers she did read from time to time had blown hot and cold for the past few years. One day there was a major crisis, the next a face-saving formula or a little mentioned climb-down and everybody got back on with their lives. Two weeks later she would see the same story, now forgotten and insulating her fish supper. This year had been no exception. Rosa vaguely recalled some fuss about Austria (or was it Czechoslovakia?)

back in the spring, just before she met George. How horrible! How fantastic! How boring.

The current crisis played out in much the same way as normal. Important people made earnest little speeches, other important people raised a counter-point or perhaps argued, in a somewhat circular manner, that they wouldn't have started from here. The Prime Minister was said to be flying to and from Germany, which sounded rather exotic to Rosa.

Occasionally the pace of trade would drop enough for Rosa to have a proper lunch break. She would walk around the town centre in search of a place to eat her sandwich and maybe compose a reply to George. It was on one such noontime that she wandered into the open-air market. As surely as people were trying to acquire all manner of items, the market traders seemed to have had fresh deliveries of goods which provided, at best, marginal utility to their prospective purchaser. Rosa made the mistake of meeting the gaze of a man who was hawking what looked to be goose grease in squat glass jars. She was reluctantly engaged in conversation. As was her habit, she couldn't bring herself to just snub the speaker, even though she really needed to be heading back to the shop.

"What is it?" enquired Rosa, pointing at one of the jars.

"It's a shock-proofing treatment for windows, glassware and other breakables." Rosa's face arranged itself into a questioning pout. The salesman smiled inwardly, he had her attention, step one in his sales patter successfully completed.

"When Gerry starts dropping bombs on us you'll be glad of this" he enthused.

"How does it work?" asked Rosa flatly, never one to avoid a direct question.

"Ah, wouldn't you like to know?" responded the salesman evasively. He now moved to step two, the science.

"When a bomb explodes, most of the damage comes from the shockwave, not the explosive. The shockwave is just a lot of sound." Rosa allowed this. It sounded plausible.

"Now, as you know a duck's quack doesn't echo." Rosa wasn't aware of this fact, but had no easy way of proving otherwise.

"Well if we take the fat from a duck and coat a fragile surface with it, the surface is protected from shockwaves." The market trader smiled as if he had just completed an elegant scientific proof. Rosa smiled back. It seemed a large, and somewhat illogical, leap of faith. She thought the most likely result of using the preparation would be an opaque window smelling of dead duck. She started to move off.

"It can also be used to make crispy roast potatoes!" he hollered, desperate now to make the sale. Rosa had now turned her back to him as he shouted after her "buy one, get one free."

Everywhere Rosa went a collective madness seemed to have gripped the population. Sensible, apparently rational adults would walk out into the road without looking. Cars, horses or bikes often missed them by fractions of an inch. General stores had run out of milk, bread and other perishables, but stocks of tinned food remained largely untouched. The general mood appeared to be that war was inevitable and that when it came it would bring swift annihilation at the hands of German airpower, probably within the hour.

The second week of Rosa's posting was now drawing to an end. For this she could find little relief, knowing that the insanity of the crowd in this town was doubtless repeated across the country. She longed now for the dull pleasure of a lonely night at the Cinema or sitting at the back of a church hall smelling the damp plaster and reading a cheap novel whilst some zealot propounded his view of the world. She longed also to be in George's company, tucked under his left arm whilst he ranted about Chamberlain or kissed her on the nose. But the immediate future was not promising any such comforts. As she awoke on Friday morning she took an aspirin from force of habit. A bad habit learned only in the past few weeks. Her stomach heaved ominously and she resolved to eat at least a slice of toast before going to work. The wireless was on in the dining room, a news program spoke to an audience hanging on its every word. Rosa felt cold. Her stomach pains were forgotten as she joined the others in the dining room. And then the fateful words.

"The Prime Minister last night concluded a settlement of the Czechoslovakian problem with the leaders of France, Italy and Germany. He is expected to have further talks with Herr Hitler this morning before returning to London."

Rosa looked at the faces in the dining room, many of them some years older than hers. The same faces that doubtless cheered in the streets as armies mobilised one summer just twenty-four years ago. Now they sat with barely suppressed glee on their faces at the prospect of peace. Was it a peace with honour? Was it peace for our time? Rosa couldn't ask the questions, never mind answer them. She knew at least it was peace for *a* time. She threw the packets of aspirins into the bin.

Peer Review

Samuel Goldsmith unlocked the door to his office and sat down heavily on his chair. He let out a sigh. It was a sigh of both relief and exhaustion. The bank manager was an old friend and had agreed to a rearrangement of the terms along the lines Samuel had requested. Samuel however could not view this as anything other than failure. The inescapable truth was that Goldsmith Chemicals Limited had run out of money. Of the industries they had approached with their new process only one, the LNER, had committed money and this had come with some very significant conditions. Their initial payment bought the salts which George had seen powering "The Republic of Great Britain". But it also bought a commitment from Goldsmith Chemicals to deliver a much larger shipment of salts by September, the price having been fixed by reference to the equivalent quantity (in calorific value) of coal. It had always been an ambitious commitment.

The weeks after concluding this transaction had been rather promising. The original assays had arrived back confirming the composition of the ore, the sediment and the salts in solution. It was a filthy mixture, as if somebody had taken the periodic table and shaken it violently. Reviewing the assays Samuel remarked the only thing missing was lizard's leg and owlet's wing. There were inevitable false starts but Jacob got to work isolating the active components. By an elaborate set of titrations, precipitations and a judicious use of filters and settling tanks he eventually arrived at a solution containing the active element. Uranium. Uncle and nephew were flushed with triumph.

Samuel dispatched orders for pitchblende whilst Jacob returned to the library to read what he could about the chemistry of Uranium. Information was fairly thin though there was coverage of its use in glassware and there were a few colour illustrations showing the yellow glazes it could impart. In the studious, conspiratorial silence of the reading rooms, where Karl Marx had written the Communist Manifesto a century ago, Jacob grappled with his own revolutionary experience, trying to put some kind of theoretical framework around the concepts he had collided with.

Uranium. Element ninety two. The last element? Or the element of last resort? Well, it had led to the discovery of x-rays. Then there were Marie Curie's adventures with pitchblende and her isolation of Radium and Polonium. Jacob had a keen enough mind and wondered if his own process had stumbled upon some analogue. Some kind of artificial radioactivity perhaps? But he also knew the limits of his own abilities. He was an engineer of some talent, but not a research scientist.

The summer brought disappointments. The cost of pitchblende was higher than had been anticipated. The processing into a pure aqueous solution was lengthy, made worse by the protective equipment they judged it necessary to wear. On days when the sun made an appearance the factory was warmed to unpleasant temperatures and work could proceed only in short shifts. The body blow came in August. By then they had a critical quantity of the aqueous solution, prepared so far in small batches to avoid the process initiating itself. Jacob introduced these batches into the larger tank and waited for the temperature to rise, but it remained stubbornly stable at 68 degrees Fahrenheit. They suspected some error, some subtle difference in chemical composition that was inhibiting the expected reaction. They commissioned fresh assays which only confirmed that they had faithfully recreated the required solution – they were chemically identical. Yet one would evolve heat and the other one was cold and inert.

All the slender resources of Goldsmith Chemicals were brought to bear on this problem. Commissions and opportunities were turned down to meet the LNER deadline of September, but by late August they still had nothing to send to Doncaster beyond the original ore. There were discussions with the railway company, who had their own misgivings about the project. With the rumours of war the prevailing mood was no longer one of innovation, but rather of consolidation. There was even talk of cooperation on new engine designs with their erstwhile rivals across the Pennines, the LMS. They offered an extension of the deadline by a month, or Goldsmith Chemicals repay the initial payment and the salts would be returned to Wimbledon.

Ultimately work had to stop on the now rather tainted "Goldsmith process". Samuel called in old favours, took whatever opportunities he could find, refinanced, and with the hard work and uncommon skill of Jacob they brought the business back from the brink by concentrating on the mundane but profitable trade of old.

The LNER returned the salts on the morning of Friday 30th September.

Cerys

The directions had been hand written. From the choice of stationary and the handwriting it was fairly obvious the author was female. Philipa's forensics skills did not stretch much further, so curiosity impelled her to look at them again. The senders address was that of the Statesman, and the letter was written as if he was addressing her, but the occasional paragraph indulged in a chatty, informal manner that was clearly not his own.

The Statesman, it explained had fallen ill. Nothing life threatening or contagious, but enough to prevent his presence in either London or Birmingham. As a consequence Philipa had been summoned to meet her patron at his family home in Cardiganshire. Directions were furnished in elaborate detail with pen work diagrams in exaggerated perspective of the milestones upon her route. The directions were broken down into chapters, each one consisting of three milestones. Each picture was signed "Cerys the Cartographer", and had a smiling roll of parchment in the top left hand corner. Mrs Arden smiled to herself. Someone had been given a mundane task, but had instead taken a day to please themselves. It was the measure of the Statesman that he should employ such characters - and indulge them in such whimsy.

Friday found Philipa on the platform at Ruabon, waiting for her next train as *Treago Castle* hauled the Birkenhead-Paddington express off into the distance. She took tea in the buffet and read rather self-consciously from a children's book recently written by an old Oxford acquaintance. She imagined herself as a character in that novel, about to embark on a quest into the mountains of the hinterland. After some minutes she broke off reading and took in her surroundings. The Great Western Railway was the regional superpower, announced in a hundred subtle ways – an etching on the glass, a motif on the fire bucket and now made glorious by the drawing into the station of her connecting train. She hurriedly finished her drink, slipped the novel into her Gladstone bag and went to board the train.

The carriages were coloured a familiar chocolate and cream and had seemed to Philipa at first to be decidedly modern, with glazed, bow ends to them. Now closer inspection showed them to be rather meanly decorated, the guiding principle presumably being to keep costs to a minimum. Philipa boarded the train and settled into her seat. She looked out of the window expectantly, surveying the small view of Ruabon that she was afforded before the train left. She was now in Wales, although outward appearances could convince her she was in the English Midlands. The station itself seemed busy and self-important, although there were very few passengers about. During the summer months it teamed as excited Midlanders entrained for the joys of the Welsh seaside at Rhyl, Portmadoc or Barmouth. Now in the depths of autumn the infrastructure was preparing for hibernation, with final coats of paint being administered by staff before the rains and frosts of Winter blew coldly in.

The minute of departure came and went. The train remained resolutely stationary. Philipa fancied perhaps that the driver and firemen were out on the pavements trying to drum up more custom. In any event no further passengers were forthcoming and the train duly departed, ten minutes late.

Llangollen arrived quickly and now Philipa had no doubt she was in Wales. She craned to look out of the windows at the towering hills, trying to pick out the ruined castle which her Baedeker had enthused about. The stop was brief, perhaps in deference to the time lost at Ruabon. The cloud had broken so that occasional spells of sunlight illuminated the journey. The train rattled along at a pleasant pace suggestive of progress without undue haste. The novel Philipa had brought with her lay unread as she drank in the scenery, which evoked images of fairy-tale knights and red dragons. She had thought of Saint George and King Arthur, but neither seemed right for this distinctly Celtic landscape. Presently the train ran through a tunnel before drawing into Corwen. Someone outside hollered that those bound for Rhyl should change here, but there were few takers. The engine heaved Philipa's train slowly on westward.

Some hours later Philipa got down from her carriage with a grateful weariness. The journey had seemed circuitous in the extreme. At the direction of Cerys the Cartographer she had broken for lunch at Bala which had lead her to a queer little fish-and-chip shop serving battered trout accompanied by an illicit bottle of cider and a strict injunction not to let the minister know. The final leg of the journey had seen her pass through Dolgellau before snaking down the coast in a vague southerly direction.

As she emerged from the station hall she saw the car sent to take her to the Statesman's house. In front of the vehicle stood a young woman dressed in brown leathers, presumably a drivers outfit although she looked rather like an aviatrix. The girl's ample form filled every corner of the outfit. She was one of those girls that vengeful maiden aunts label plump, although she had clearly attracted the attention of the male railway staff. She greeted Philipa in an accent which betrayed little aside from the occasional Welsh lilt.

"I'm Myfanwy, but you can call me Myffy."

"Philipa. Philipa Arden. Pleased to meet you. Would that be Myfanwy as in...."

"Yes, the very same, errant daughter, personal secretary, driver and anything else that advances the Liberal cause."

"I like your outfit" commented Philipa genuinely. Myfanwy involuntarily ran a hand from just under her bust, down her torso and onto her thighs, a prideful look on her face. She bit her lip, a self-denying Narcissus. A change of subject was called for.

"You're not what I expected. I thought you'd be some dreary Victorian governess."

"And instead you got Mary Poppins?" jibed Philipa.

"I do hope so!" and Myfanwy threw Philipa's carpet bag into the boot of the car. Philipa placed the smaller Gladstone in herself. They were soon seated in the car and Myfanwy took off from the station at a tremendous rate. Philipa could see the flying suit was entirely appropriate.

"Was it you who wrote my directions?" enquired Philipa. Myfanwy blushed.

"No. That was Cerys the Cartographer" she replied impishly. Cerys the Cartographer took rather too liberal an approach to the next bend, and Philipa clutched at the door handle. It didn't make the journey any safer, but she saw it as a talisman jointly to St Christopher and St Jude. Travel and lost causes. *Croeso i fy buchedd.*

After little more than a mile the car had climbed high up into the hills above the town and soon drew up at the family home. The house itself was unimpressive, although the view was rather stunning.

Philipa took it in as Myfanwy took the luggage out of the car. She could see down to the ribbon of the town some hundreds of feet below. Cardigan bay crashed in small wavelets all along the coast, visible for several miles before disappearing into the river estuary to the North. To her right, further inland, flat marshland occupied most of the field of vision. Directly ahead of her, but in the background on the other side of the estuary, gaily painted houses stood out as the individuals that they were along a shoreline that rose quickly into impressive hills, featureless only because of the distance and the clouds that were now rolling up to cover them.

Autumn Song

A headline from an old newspaper reads "Great Powers Renounce War", dated August 28th 1928. There's a picture taken in the East Room of the White House. George struggles to identify most of those pictured but there's Cal Coolidge and maybe that smudge is Herbert Hoover. The rest are long forgotten ambassadors and foreign ministers. Something called the Kellogg-Briand Pact, forgotten now in all the noise of the past few years. It was an honourable attempt. And it encouraged a degree of optimism for a while.

This particular headline had prompted George to start collecting newspapers, whenever the story looked to be suitably historic. He surveyed his modest collection now. There was the Wall Street crash and then a gap of some years before the headlines ushering in the debacle of 1931 and the National Government. There was nothing about Hitler until mid-1934, an omission on George's part, but then he shared that guilt with plenty of others. He had not one, but two papers from 'thirty-five covering some piece of nonsense called the Stresa Conference in which Mussolini had tried his hand as a peace maker, even as he schemed in private against Abyssinia.

George searched through his papers, but it seemed he had missed the initial invasion of Abyssinia. The only reference to it was a dispatch from a Red Cross camp some months later which didn't spare the reader the suffering and made difficult reading even at this distance. The collection was more successful at recording the Rhineland remilitarization, and the civil war in Spain, which confused George even now. He could just about grasp the essential conflict between Franco's Fascists and the left-wing Republicans, but beyond that lay pages of broadsheet bluster, contradiction and incoherent self-interest.

The final omission from George's inglorious collection was the absence of the Abdication. He did have news of the old King's death. Indeed he would admit to a certain sentimental fondness for George V. But all the squalid conspiracies and plain reaction that had unseated hapless Edward had bored him so much he had thrown the abdication special out in temper.

Thus were ended his ambitions to sequester history into a cardboard box. He hadn't bothered to record the kerfuffle over the annexation of Austria back in March nor for that matter the Munich Agreement from a few weeks ago. They seemed to be just variations on a theme, and if war did come then a score of newspapers, unread for some time and yellowing already, would hardly make things any better. Munich and the Sudetenland. George tried not to dwell on this. His feelings were an ambivalent mess.

He pulled out another old paper, this one from 'thirty-three. He flipped to the sports pages. There was all the controversy, the English use of the "fast leg theory" in the Ashes tour. Some hot-head had christened it "Bodyline Bowling" which made it seem unsporting. George recalled that he had seen it as a legitimate tactic at the time, but now he had to admit that it was, as they say, "not cricket".

George sniffed at the broadsheet and savoured the smell of printers ink and old paper. It recalled a recurrent dream which has plagued him for almost a decade. We stand at the brow of a hill, looking down on a forest fire. We can smell the wood smoke, can hear the crackle of timber and see the angry amber torment of the flames. But we are at a safe distance. Only gradually do we realise that the fire is advancing towards us. At first the progress seems glacial in its slowness but it has deceived us and there comes a definite point at which we realise the advance is a real danger. We are no longer idle spectators, but victims and we mourn this fall in status. But still we can barely tear our eyes from the awful sight, observing the destruction with a detached, perhaps a morbid, fascination. And then a change of wind direction and the fire is checked. But there had been that desperate rush of adrenalin, the memory of which will last much longer than the event itself.

None of this was helping him to find his birth certificate. He had been searching for it for the greater part of the afternoon. George dimly remembered receiving it in the post from his Mother some years ago. He remembered putting it away somewhere secure, certain that there would be a time in the future when he might need it again. But that was where his powers of recollection stopped. The building society had been quite clear that they needed to see it before they could come to a conclusion about George's creditworthiness. And he simply had to have that house. Though it probably meant abandoning any hope of owning the MG, he had to have it. It was in a nice part of town, where the trees have matured a little and the initial redbrick had mellowed. It was keenly priced, but it was the look of the place that had grabbed him. You know how you sometimes look at a girl and know instinctively that you will fall for her? And when you look again she's smiling in a different way or maybe frowning, and yet you're still smitten? As it had been with Rosa, so it was with this house. George hadn't quite made the leap of faith that conjugated these two desirables together, but he pictured showing Rosa around:

"Very nice my love" she says in measured tones.
"Do you really like it?"
"It's very nice" she replies, damning by faint praise.
"You don't like it."
"No. It's a fine house. You must be very proud."
"I'm pleased with it."
"Well that's good then, isn't it?"
"What's up?"
"Nothing." Rosa smiles the thinnest of smiles.
"Will you help me decorate?"
"If you'd like me to."
"I would" confesses George.
"Then I will."
"That would be nice." Nice, that damnable adjective again!
"You need some furniture."

"I do. My folks will lend me a few sticks, and Mrs Minshull has insisted on giving me an occasional table."

"And some curtains. You need some curtains."

"Of course" but in George's mind he's wishing she'd just follow his lead and be happy in this moment. Curtains indeed!

"The place needs a woman's touch" she suggests, dipping a metaphoric toe into an unexplored pool. The water seems icy cold but one might get used to it with time.

"I'd value your opinion."

"But would you act on it?" She asks candidly. Silence from George, a smile and a disarming shrug. It's charming even as it's annoying.

"Would you like to see upstairs?" He asks.
"Steady on my love!"

"Since I have neither curtains nor bedroom furniture I think you're safe."

"I'll trust you at your word." But, she thinks, sometimes a bit of danger would be nice. How typical of a good middle-class boy that an absence of furniture would be enough to dampen his ardour! They climb the stairs and are given a view of the rear of the property. The abundant foliage of the trees is a palette of orange and gold.

"Oh George, what a beautiful garden."

"It is rather nice isn't it?"

They walk into the bedroom and can see down into the gardens either side. Two children are playing, heedless of the world around them, their play a glorious antidote to worldly cynicism and bitter experience.

"Do you think you'll be happy here?" she asks, a loaded question if ever there was one.

"Do you?" he asks and watches the implications of this reciprocation unfold upon her face.

It's a bold move, but autumn is the time for bold moves. Leaving home, going to University, getting a job – events that open up possibilities simultaneously frightening and exciting. The house seems the next logical step, but even after this there are other firsts to chalk up. It might be corny beyond belief, it's certainly at odds with everything the weekend papers have led him to believe but George has an inkling that the best times have yet to come. Away from daydreams, back in his rented room at Mrs Minshull's, he continues to search for the birth certificate upon which so much is dependant.

The Statesman

The Statesman was asleep in the study as Myfanwy ushered Philipa through. A book was open and face down across his chest. The smell of pipe tobacco hung in the air. The old man before her was only a palimpsest of the man she had known since her youth.

"I'm sorry" mouthed Myfanwy silently and walked over to him.

"Dad. Dad. Wake up." Myfanwy prodded her father with a hesitant finger. He remained motionless.

"Daddy" Myfanwy called rather more tenderly. The Statesman stirred.

"Dora. Has Dora escaped the Bolshies?" he mumbled.

"Daddy, it's Myffy. Mrs Arden has arrived." He orientated himself and flushed with embarrassment. He arose and closed the book, putting it on the arm of the chair, then strode over to greet Philipa. As he crossed the room the transformation was profound. The weary, dozing antiquity had lost a clear twenty years. Philipa beamed delightedly at the resurrection.

"Philipa. I'm so pleased to see you."

"It's an honour to be invited to your home."

"A necessity I'm afraid. The quack has forbidden me to travel for the next few weeks. I'm sure Myffy has acquainted you with the dreadful details." He paused and looked at his watch. "Time for tea and bara brith?" He asked hopefully. Myfanwy retreated to the kitchen and prepared afternoon tea.

The late afternoon passed in happy conversation, the Statesman clearly energised by the attentions of two younger women. They remained in the study. There was only one easy chair which had been first offered to Philipa, and then Myfanwy, but they had both declined, sitting instead at his feet and before the open fire. There, staring up at a man she had admired for the greater part of her life, Philipa felt an absurd sense of belonging, but to whom or what she was unsure.

As the evening drew in Myfanwy made reluctant preparations to go out. A hapless young man arrived to collect her, but was corralled into being the passenger in Myffy's MG. Philipa and the

Statesman had been left a simple evening meal by the housekeeper. They ate in the dining room which enjoyed the view over Cardigan Bay. Philipa admired the view to the north west and was informed it was the Llyn peninsula.

"Do you remember the fuss a couple of years ago about Saunders Lewis?" Philipa did not.

"Up there used to sit a farmhouse, Penyberth. Nothing grand, but home to generations of poets and their patrons. The Air Ministry got it into their heads they were going to build a bombing range there."

"A sign of the times I suppose" said Philipa.

"Well they got up a delegation to see Mr Baldwin. It's said they'd got half a million signatures. But the stuffed shirt refused to see them, although he'd been quick enough to back off plans for the same in Dorset and Northumberland." Philipa leant forward, the old man was back in his pre-war form.

"I wrote a personal letter to him. Never even got a reply. As a final insult they started work on the four hundredth anniversary of the act of union." Philipa was wide-eyed. Back in thirty-six she'd heard nothing of this, all she could remember was the abdication and the troubles in Spain.

"Well the mood was thunderous. There was a lot of talk of resistance, but none of it amounted to much. That was until sometime in the autumn. Someone got in and set fire to the Aerodrome buildings. The crime was brought home to Lewis and two other chaps, Valentine and Williams. They're prime movers in the Welsh nationalist movement." Philipa giggled. The Statesman stopped talking and looked at her like a disapproving school teacher.

"*Welsh* nationalism, you're pulling my leg?" And she was certain he was.

"I can assure you I'm not." With enormous effort Philipa contained her mirth.

"The three of them were rather proud of what they'd done. There was a trial in Caernarfon, which couldn't reach a verdict. There was a further trial in London where the accused demanded to be heard in Welsh, and the Judge walked into the trap of insisting on English. And that was that. They were sent to Wormwood Scrubs for 9 months and achieved martyrdom."

"I never realised feelings ran so strongly." Philipa conceded.

"Neither did I until the other year. I think it's woken a lot of us up in this neck of the woods."

"So the natives are restless?" suggested Philipa.

"Oh the movement, such as it is, is all rather chaotic. There are those that are in it to preserve the Welsh language, some, like Mr Lewis who seek a wider cultural revival. And of course there are the rabble-rousers and zealots."

"Are you involved? If you don't mind me asking?"

"Good lord. No doubt you think I've gone native? No, I'm not involved. Just a professional interest. Myffy flirted with it for a while. She honed her Welsh expounding self-determination and the labour theory of value."

"Do Marxist economics sound any better in Welsh?" asked Philipa laconically.

"They don't make any more sense, but it sounds delightful. Unfortunately she was addressing the Sunday school class at the time". Talk rambled from the political to the personal and back again. There was an easy, unforced air to the conversation that Philipa's previous meetings had not had. They touched on Philipa's research, and Philipa summoned the courage to ask a question that had troubled her since taking the commission.

"What relevance do you suppose the concept of a night watchman state has these days?"

"Steady on! That's a big question for this late in an evening." He looked longingly at his pipe, but dismissed an urge to relight it. "I suppose you have in mind the popular belief that laissez-faire economics finished sometime in 'thirty-one?"

"I think the popular word is "discredited" rather than "finished"" she smiled, hoping he would appreciate the scholarly nature of her enquiry, and also hoping that she hadn't offended him.

"Well, I would make two observations." He took a draft of his wine. It was an inferior, if more sociable, alternative to his tobacco.

"Firstly, I would argue that our problems in the past two decades have not been caused by *lack* of intervention by Government. It takes a particular kind of administrative meddling to engineer the debacle of our return to, and then ignominious exit from, the gold standard. And what goes for the British Empire is just as true for Germany or America." Philipa smiled, she had been right to broach the question. The old man fizzed with life.

"Secondly, my idea of a night watchman state is rather more pragmatic than the theorists would have you believe. Sometimes the defence of the realm demands a degree of intervention. When markets are seized by a collective insanity is it not the duty of the state to try to restore order? It obviously has to be measured, and it has to be specific. And most of all it has to be temporary. But it is entirely consistent with the principles of a night watchman state." There was the briefest of pauses for breath, before he continued.

"Finally, and I know I promised only two observations but this is important. I think too much is made of the economics and not enough about the quality of our lives. Of course it is important that people have food and shelter, and indeed employment. But in the past few decades we seem to have lost sight of the most important thing – the ability just to get on with living our lives without being told what to do, where to go or when to do it. The concept of individual liberty is hardly talked about. I think most of us in this country still value it. It has never been under more threat and yet we fuss instead over percentages of this or that." He stopped and took a fresh draft of his wine. Philipa was partially satisfied. She might have enquired more deeply but also wanted his opinion on more recent events.

"What do you make of the Czech business?" she ventured.

"I wondered when we'd get to that." He leant over to top up Philipa's wine glass, but the bottle was empty. "Shall we go through to the study?" The hall between dining room and study was dark now and they proceeded cautiously to avoid the household obstacles that halls gain down the years. In the study the Statesman went over to a bookshelf. He pulled out a large atlas, the dust jacket absent and the writing on the spine faded from much thumbing. He then pulled out a similarly proportioned envelope and retrieved a map from within.

Philipa was admiring a framed caricature of the Statesman on the wall. It appeared to be the original, drafted in ink on flimsy looking paper. The Statesman was dressed in a black outfit, complete with black cape and a black eye mask. It was a cartoon representation of a late nineteenth-century anarchist. He held in one hand the ubiquitous spherical bomb, with the flame having burnt halfway down the fuse. With the other hand he was rather expertly extinguishing the flame between thumb and forefinger. The artist's signature was partly obscured by the frame. She looked over at the Statesman for an answer.

"Bukharin" he said in a rather matter of fact manner, looking up only briefly.

"The Russian?"

"Indeed. It was sent to me sometime in the twenties. I corresponded with him for a while."

"No wonder they shot him" remarked Philipa, feeling rather clever but also a touch callous.

"Quite" he replied without judgement. He busied himself with the maps, opening them at the requisite pages. Finally he waved his hand with a flourish.

"There we are my dear, all of Central Europe at your feet." Philipa held her hands together and looked up at her patron in mock gratitude.

"I'd have settled for a glass of port and another slice of the bara brith."

"We must all make sacrifices." He cleared his throat and lit his pipe

"The first question we have to ask is are we prepared to go to war in the next year or two? Or would we be in a better position to engage our enemies in five or ten years' time?"

"Do we really have that choice?" asked Philipa

"A reasonable enquiry, but bear with me for a moment."

"Now, if you allow that we would rather fight in the next year or two then I agree that Munich was a disaster. I would go so far as to agree with Mr Churchill that it was the first significant defeat in this next war. Czechoslovakia has a modern, well trained army. It has over a thousand aircraft and it had good defensible positions from which to attack the German homeland. Until we threw them away at the card table. Now they are gone it is only a matter of time before the whole country is a German puppet." Philipa nodded in agreement. He had echoed her view of the past few months.

"However." There was a brief pause as the Statesman passed a glass of port to Philipa. "If we would rather avoid any fight for five or ten years then we need to make some accommodations. Some pretty unpalatable accommodations. This brings me to my second question: Who are our enemies?"

"Well Germany obviously" Philipa replied, the Statesman gestured for her to continue.

"Italy. And Spain maybe." another conjure of the Statesman's hands. Half a point for each of these but not the answer he was looking for. She thought further

"Japan in the Far East" she conceded.

"What about Russia?"

"Do you think they're a threat?" It wasn't a line of thought Philipa had explored. She clung to the romantic ideal of the revolution even now as its heroes were being shot one by one in the cellars of the NKVD.

"Don't worry, my dear, I haven't become a red-baiter in my dotage. Whilst I'd sooner not choose between the bolshies and the fascists, I will acknowledge that communism starts with more noble intentions. It does at least admit we share a common humanity, whilst fascism tries to deny such a thing."

"You know where my sympathies lie. And that's why I ask: Do you honestly think the Russians are a threat?" insisted Philipa.

"If we're thinking of a decade on from now then we have to take them seriously. In any event we have to accept Germany, Russia and Japan as they are. We have to get on with them and mobilize what support there is for containing them. We need to rid ourselves of the idea that a war with Germany is inevitable. In the next ten years it is just as plausible we might have to contain Russia, perhaps in Finland, or Persia or even in the Far East. We would need to negotiate away third parties territories that are not of strategic interest." At this he waved his hand casually around the map taking in first Asia Minor, then the Baltic and finally the Balkans.

"We would play one power off against the other. Exploit their own paranoia. All the while, as we sell them steel to make battleships and woollen goods to clothe their armies, as we extend them sterling credits and dine politely with their diplomats we would be building up our Empire, ensuring that for at least one quarter of the world an enlightened and peaceful power rules."

"Perfidious Albion" breathed Philipa, taking a small sip from her port.

"Why perfidious? The Czechs and others would know where they stood. They would know that we make no pretensions to be the world's policeman. Czechoslovakia was born of a desire for self-determination fanned by Woodrow Wilson and the United States. If the United States can stand aloof in their hour of need, why not Britain?"

"Because we're better than that" she said. It came from the heart. It wasn't a reasoned response. Something in her upbringing taught her this was wrong. That you had to stand up to the tap room bully. But she couldn't frame it any more eloquently.

"What course would you take?" asked Philipa in exasperation.

"I really don't know. The only real grounds for our intervention would be a German strike against the Low Countries or an unprovoked attack on France. Making a stand on any other front would be an exercise in futility. To give determined resistance in Czechoslovakia or anywhere in Eastern Europe requires a strong ally in the east. I suppose we might yet conclude an agreement with the Russians. Stranger things have happened. But after Munich I doubt they have much time for us" answered the Statesman sadly.

"Surely you're not tempted by the long game?"

"No, but I'm not very tempted by the short one either. Do you really want another conflict like the Great War? Because make no mistake it would be a war of attrition. Take any measure you choose – steel or aircraft production, birth rate, agriculture. You'll see how finely balanced the two sides are. There isn't a hope it would be over by this Christmas or the next. Or indeed the one after that."

"But you're the Statesman. You must know!" she protested dramatically. It was an attempt to lighten the mood but it felt hollow even as the words left her mouth.

"Are you familiar with the Internationale?"

"The..." Philipa wasn't certain what he was talking about.

"The song. It's an old left wing hymn. I believe it's the national anthem of the Soviet Union."

"Vaguely."

"The English translation is pretty dreadful, but it has the most marvellous line in its second or third stanza - *No saviour from on high delivers, no trust have we in Prince or Peer.*"

"I like that. It could have been written by the Night Watchman."

"Indeed" agreed the Statesman, somewhat uncomfortably. Philipa was about to enquire about his discomfort when Myfanwy returned.

"We have much to discuss tomorrow. With Inspector Kaye."

The Night Watchman

Philipa had got to bed about midnight and slept soundly until a heavy aircraft buzzed overhead at about six. She returned to a more shallow sleep entertained by a series of wild dreams that appeared improbable even to her unconscious mind. The final sequence had her sat in the passenger seat of Myffy's MG, the roof down on a warm summer's day as Inspector Kaye chased them across the Welsh desert. As they drove on, not daring to stop, further police cars joined the pursuit. Myfanwy's prowess at driving established a clear distance between the pair and the police, but they found themselves trapped on a high plateau, a police cordon now converging on them from three sides. The remaining side was a sheer drop, some hundreds of feet into oblivion. Myffy stopped.

"What now?" asked Philipa. Surrender wasn't an option.

"Let's just keep driving" suggested Myfanwy.

"Let's do it." And they looked deeply into each other's eyes. A bond of universal sisterhood, no doubt, but also more. "One of us should say something" thought Philipa, but there was only the sound of the converging police and the surging engine in the MG. They drove into the abyss.

Philipa was woken sharply by a tap at the door.

"Cup of tea?" Ventured Myfanwy, peering round the door and proffering a cup and saucer

"Oh thank you" answered Philipa sleepily.

"I've got to do some work on the car this morning, but we could go for a drive this afternoon if you're finished in time."

"That would be lovely" Philipa replied.

"Can I do anything else for you?" Philipa responded politely in the negative.

Breakfast was taken in the dining room. The day had started clear, but the sky was rapidly clouding over and the view of the coast was diminishing by the hour. The housekeeper was fussing around making sure everything was in order for the Inspector's arrival. The Statesman was dressed casually, exuding an air of calm that was reflected in the tranquillity within. Myfanwy defiantly sported a boiler suit, fired by a youthful wariness of the state's servants and past encounters between favourite clothing and Castrol engine oil. Philipa had dressed for business, curious at last to meet the policeman who had shown such an interest in her research.

Kaye arrived by car just before 10 and they received him in the study, additional easy chairs having been brought through for their meeting. Myfanwy made her excuses and went to service the car.

"Thank you for receiving me at your home sir" began the Inspector. The air of deference made all present rather uncomfortable.

"Don't mention it, and please dispense with the "Sir" nonsense. You are my guest, so I would much prefer you call me Edward."

"Thank you." Replied the Inspector "I hope not to take too much of your time. I am here in an unofficial capacity. As I mentioned in my letter I would like to discuss your interest in the Night Watchman. I would also like to share with you what I know, my concerns and come to an agreement with you. Until we have reached an agreement I would ask that all the discussions we have remain confidential."

"You have my word" replied the Statesman.

"And mine too" added Philipa.

"Philipa, perhaps you would care to tell the Inspector what we know."

"Certainly. My research has brought up anecdotes and legend about a group called the Night Watchman. They are primarily an English affair, with very little penetration into Scottish, Welsh or Irish folklore." Philipa paused and glanced at her written notes. She had a professional concern that she didn't overlook any fact.

"Their reason for being is undetermined, but there is strong secondary evidence that they are against an over bearing state and very much in favour of individual liberties. Their origin is unknown, but dates back at least to sometime in the 17th Century." She paused again. The bullet points had all been covered, the remaining substance of her work was the details of the anecdotes. From these tales she had constructed an interpretation of their motives and goals, but it was supposition and she was unhappy repeating that to the Inspector.

"I could take you through some of the recurrent themes within the tales I have uncovered?" she suggested.

"I may take you up on that later, but it won't be necessary at this point" replied Kaye "Would you care to take me through the modern day practice of the Night Watchman."

"I'm not sure I can help you, there is no canon of this organisation. There is no organisation in existence today."

"What about those you have met with who claim to be its adherents. Mr Maxwell for example." Philipa smiled, confident she could reassure the Inspector.

"Oh, they're just overgrown school boys following some kind of comic book secret society nonsense." She smiled disarmingly, but Kaye was not reassured.

"I wish that were the truth. My job acquaints me with organisations of every flavour and persuasion. I know what makes them tick. Nothing pleases me more than leaving most of them alone. However the current adherents to the Night Watchman show some rather worrying tendencies."

"Such as?" The Statesman enquired.

"A large degree of coordination. A commonly acknowledged leader of considerable charisma. A foothold in our most strategically important industries and an increasing appetite for activities that come close to insurrection." Philipa was stony faced. It was true that Maxwell and some others seemed increasingly taken with direct action. Insurrection? That was laying it on a bit thick. Philipa let it stand but issued a rebuttal to the blatant untruths.

"Who is this "charismatic leader?" I'm not aware of him. I have found no such leader" she declared defiantly.

"Do you really not know, Mrs Arden? Why it's you. You are the one they all look to. You have created this movement." Philipa was speechless. She didn't know where to start to unpick this. Her eyes searched wildly across the face of the Inspector and then the Statesman.

"I haven't done anything to encourage this" Philipa insisted at last. The Inspector looked at her with a degree of incredulity. The Statesman examined the bottom of his tea cup.

"I don't think Inspector Kaye is suggesting you have deliberately orchestrated this." replied the Statesman gently "Are you, Francis?" he added more firmly.

"I am not making such an accusation." He conceded grudgingly "Rather, that your research has had an unexpected consequence. That the very act of looking for this extinct organisation has brought to life a different, rather virulent group. Now the question we face is what to do about it." There was a pause, all present wondering who should speak next, weighing their next words so that they would be unambiguous.

"We could use it" whispered Philipa suddenly struck by an idea. "Edward, we could use this to breath fire into the old party. Imagine a movement with all these people of action behind it? Imagine what we could do with their enthusiasm? Their vitality! The ends they strive for are substantially the same as ours!" she finished in a gasp, short of breath from the excitement.

"I feared this might be your reaction" Inspector Kaye observed quietly. More silence. Only the muffled sound of thoroughly modern Myffy working on the MG. The Statesman eventually spoke.

"Philipa. Do you suppose that this country, or indeed the wider world, really needs another messianic cult? I don't need to imagine what such a movement would look like. I only have to look at Rome or Berlin to see where your men of action would take us."

"There's no reason why we would make their mistakes" she protested, but Philipa knew instinctively that the Statesman was right. In the twenties she had studied Oswald Mosely, a talented Labour minister seduced by the pursuit of pure power. Now he was more a machine than a man. For both Philipa and the Statesman progress meant the blossoming of the human spirit, not some statistical conjuring around the greatest good for the greatest number. A fresh silence fell on the room as the Inspector reached into his briefcase and removed a series of dossiers.

"I mentioned earlier that I would like us to arrive at an agreement. I have a proposal for the two of you which I would like to outline." Neither Philipa nor the Statesman objected.

"The Night Watchman does indeed date back to the 17th Century, Its existence is acknowledged in a series of documents I have, dated from 1649 onwards. It starts with a field communication to Thomas Fairfax, one of Cromwell's generals. It describes them in much the same terms as folklore remembers them."

"Sixteen Forty Nine. The early days of Cromwell's Commonwealth. All those dissenters and my Night Watchman are part of it." Philipa felt a flush of maternal pride.

"As far as I know the documents I have are the only primary sources to describe them. From the way they are described it would seem that the Night Watchman are as much a part of the English dissenting tradition as any of the dozen or so other groups of that time."

"And what company to keep!" rejoined Philipa "Quakers, Baptists, Levellers, Diggers, Ranters. It all makes such perfect sense." And then she stopped, suspicion rising within her.

"This could, of course, be a fake."

"You haven't seen the sheer quantity of this stuff. Nor have you seen the day to day minutiae within it. If it's all been fabricated somebody has gone to a lot of trouble. But that brings me to my proposal. I would like to give this to you for examination. You can do all the investigations you like against it. I am told modern science can put a date to paper and ink and such like. And, should you be satisfied as to the authenticity, you would be free to publish it as part of your research." The Inspector sat back in his chair and sipped his tea.

Philipa wanted to believe but was still unconvinced. "Why didn't this turn up when I did my investigations. I took enormous care to trawl the public records."

"Some public records are more public than others" commented the Statesman cryptically, informed by his own experience in public office.

"Yet another question would be why would their existence have been suppressed?" continued Philipa, willing to be convinced, but wary still about the Inspector's good faith.

"Oh somebody probably stood to lose money or face. The usual reasons" mused the Statesman lazily.

"It's possible" said the Inspector, his countenance still deferential, but suggestive also that he wasn't so easily persuaded. It might be an act, but Philipa thought not.

"Francis?" asked the Statesman with a smile. The Inspector looked at Mrs Arden. For a moment they were of the same mind. And why not? For they had now the same inputs. The game could at last be enumerated.

“I think the Inspector has reached his own conclusion, but fears he might have caught the paranoia of the true dissenter” said Philipa. The Inspector smiled weakly. The Statesman smiled too. Their three minds were as one, but it was the Statesman who spoke.

“For after all, isn’t the Night Watchman the most dangerous of all conspiracies? A conspiracy amongst the powerful not to exercise that power. These men, the New Model Army, have seen their homeland wracked by unimaginable bloodshed. In the aftermath of the bloodiest conflict to date this group, The Night Watchman, arises and proposes *not* to take control, but rather to limit the ability of *anyone* to assume control. To impose a minimalist state, and all the personal responsibility that implies. True liberty? Yes. But also true blasphemy. You can imagine the connivance of all sides in their suppression” said the Statesman, pausing for thought and breath. Nobody rushed to occupy the vacuum so left and after a long few seconds he resumed “But, and here’s the deuce of the thing, could it remain suppressed for nearly three hundred years?”

“Not suppressed, no. But ill remembered? Spoken of only as folklore? A vague hope for a better way of ordering human affairs? That’s possible” conceded Philipa. “You will recall that the Putney Debates remained unknown until the fag-end of the last century. And indeed there’s still doubt as to whether the Ranters existed. I have heard it suggested that they were just some bogeyman story got up to discredit the real dissenters. This will all need more research. But, in principle, it’s possible. I’m interested.”

“If we took these documents do I need to ask exactly what you would require in return?” The Statesman enquired, arms crossed unconsciously.

“Only that you and Mrs Arden will assist me in neutralising the organisation you have unwittingly brought into existence” said the Inspector.

“And so the cycle continues” whispered Philipa, with the vaguest feeling of becoming an accomplice in a further act of suppression. Surely, then, all the more reason to get this published? But what a choice.

“What, exactly do you mean by “neutralise”?” demanded the Statesman.

“I will not betray these people, my friends. They are of sound character with sincerely held beliefs” declared Philipa primly.

"Perhaps my choice of words was melodramatic. I have in mind an orderly disengagement. I suggest Mrs Arden ceases her contact with the individuals concerned." He turned to Philipa and added "You would make one more visit to each of them, suggesting your research is now at an end. You would rubbish any idea of a continuing movement."

"How can you be sure that would be the end of it?"

"Remember, Mrs Arden, that you are the only thing linking these disparate groups. Without your leadership they will be uncoordinated, directionless. Indistinguishable from a score of other radical organisations, and no more of a threat."

"It really is for the best." The Inspector was now almost apologetic. He sensed he was on the cusp of an agreement. However the conversation continued for some time with both the Statesman and Philipa determined to tease out all of the details. The Inspector was specific with his answers, and so many questions were necessary.

They finally reached an agreement sometime after one.

Binding Energy

Goldsmith Chemicals did rather well out of the war-that-never-was. Across the country inventories swelled in anticipation of hostilities breaking out. As these materials proved not to be required some were sold on at a discount. Enter Samuel Goldsmith. As winter established itself Samuel saw with satisfaction that the debts were being serviced and the balance sheet was in reasonable shape. It would be a long way back to rude financial good health but the company was saved from collapse.

They were left with only one remaining question: What to do with the uranium salts?

The events of the summer had demonstrated there was something remarkable about them. On those rare occasions when the pace of work would slacken both Jacob and Samuel would speculate as to what immortal hand had fashioned such a quixotic material. What pinch of fairy dust animated these salts, but not the identical ones assembled by their own futile labour? Speculation was tempered, however, by the near-death experience of their business. They would quickly return to work, determinedly dismissing this and muttering a little manta they had arrived at together "Fools Gold and Phlogiston".

There was nonetheless a need to reach a decision on the salts. They occupied a significant amount of space, which limited the ability to handle revenue earning materials. They were a proven source of considerable energy. And all the while there was the concern that the State might become interested in them. After Munich, Samuel's wariness of the British government had turned to outright disgust.

"It's like some biblical morality tale. We are required to make a judgement that Solomon would have found daunting" exclaimed the old man.

"Or Abraham at the altar with Isaac" piped up his nephew.

"Heaven knows there have been plenty of times this year when I've been tempted to do unto you that which Isaac was spared by the Almighty" the old man taunted. Jacob made a sparring punch at his Uncle's upper arm. They each took a mince pie from the packet

Samuel had bought. There was silence for a moment as they chewed away.

"It has occurred to me we could use this to raise our own steam. We'd save a fortune on coal" muttered Jacob through a mouthful of food.

"I had the same thought, but we'd still have the rotten stuff on the premises, and too many people know about it. There's bound to be unwelcome attention from somebody or other, if only from the coal merchant as we stop buying from him." Both men were silent once more, deep in thought.

"Well we can't sell it or give it away. There's too much of a risk that somebody else would discover the process. Fully developed and in the wrong hands it might be unstoppable."

"That leaves only one option" added Samuel.

"I know" admitted Jacob.

They went to their duty. Rather fittingly the winter sun peeped through the London smog and illumed their temple as they opened the valves at the base of the tanks containing the salt solution. They drained slowly, enough time for any change of heart in either of them. Enough time to close the valves. But there was no change of heart. By the evening the tanks were empty. The salts mingled with the brown waters of the Thames and flowed out into the North Sea.

Jacob looked at the blackboard on which they had speculated about the now dispersed salt. Allotrope, Isotope, Radical, Isomer, Ion. They were just words thrown up from their own memories and experience. To explore in any direction would require resources they didn't have. Jacob swept the chalk writing away with a right-left-right action. Even had his gaze lingered on the word isotope, it would have profited him nothing. For which isotope was it? And, even if he were to discover, though stroke of luck or divine inspiration, which one, nothing would have been achieved. He would need to enquire into the precise composition, to understand what enlivens the one and not the other. The differences are so marginal. It would be beyond his equipment and even his considerable skills. No, it wouldn't matter that he understood all the mysteries and had all knowledge. It would be for nothing, because it would only be knowledge in part. The slate is wiped clean, the temple is locked and if, as evening establishes itself, Jacob looks ruefully out of his Uncle's car window it is not in expectation of any message from afar.

At about the same time as Goldsmith Chemicals staged a Lazarus-like recovery, Lise Meitner journeys to Copenhagen to meet Otto Hahn. Their discussions cover many topics. Perhaps they talk of her exile and new life in Sweden, or of the recent violence of Kristallnacht. History will only record that they certainly talk of their work together. For, despite their geographic separation, they are planning a new series of experiments. They are investigating what happens when uranium is bombarded with neutrons.

As November gives way to December the experiments are performed at the Kaiser Wilhelm Institute in Berlin. Hahn keeps Meitner informed by correspondence, excitedly telling of the latest results. As the holiday approaches he and his pupil Strassmann have proven that uranium, when bombarded with a neutron, can burst open like a poorly wrapped Christmas present, disgorging lighter nuclei such as barium and krypton and an enormous quantity of energy. On hearing the news Lise marvels at the chemistry. She will later describe it as “excellent” but really there are no superlatives, in English or in German, that she felt would do justice to the achievement.

In the months to come Lise will make her own remarkable contribution by constructing the theoretical explanation for this new phenomenon. And her nephew, Otto Frisch, will grant the process its memorable name. Nuclear Fission.

Robinson Crusoe

There is something delightful about having a girl on your arm as Christmas approaches. No matter how curmudgeonly or scrooge-like your view of the festive period, to have the company of a sweetheart as the days grow shorter and the shops fill with frivolous tat is bliss itself. George had always been rather late getting into the Christmas spirit. Presents were typically bought in a hurry in the final week. Cards were often not sent at all, or fired off in a salvo a day after the last post, arriving at their destination only as the New Year approached and the recipients were eating left-over turkey.

This year Christmas started on Friday 2nd December. A card from Rosa arrived before breakfast. It was a big card, only just able to fit through Mrs Minshull's letter box. George opened it at the breakfast table with his landlady making every effort to look disinterested, but secretly wanting to submit it to her considerable investigative skills. On the front were two robins on a snow covered branch, whilst inside was a heartfelt, if rather sentimental verse and Rosa's large handwriting. It signed off with "All my love, Rosa."

"Looks like the girl is smitten" observed Mrs Minshull, unable to contain herself. George blushed a crimson colour.

"And I would say that you were too?" She ventured with a smile but also an inquisitorial look that wouldn't have looked out of place on Inspector Kaye.

"It's just a Christmas card" mumbled George, tucking into his cornflakes but mulling over Mrs Minshull's speculation.

"And the rest! You could do a lot worse than make an honest woman of that girl. She's not fast like that Mrs Arden" shouted Mrs Minshull as she departed into the larder, some chore involving dripping, offal or tallow needing her urgent attention.

With the shops being busy in the run up to Christmas they saw each other only on Sundays, and even then only because one or the other of them journeyed halfway across the railway network. Relief was, however, at hand.

"I'm being posted back to Liverpool for the last two weeks of December" chirped Rosa as George kissed her in greeting. Her face, pink and cold from the winter air, seemed even more vivacious than normal. George's mind performed a lookup in his own mental Bradshaw's A to Z. If he caught the express Liverpool was less than an hour away. The last train back to Crewe wasn't until 29 minutes past midnight. George beamed in delight and squeezed Rosa in a bear hug. George decided to ask a question that had been running through his mind for some days now. He was worried it might be too presumptuous. That he might offend her and their blossoming relationship might wither before it really began.

"Rosa, I have a question to ask, and I hope you won't be offended. And by all means say no if you think it's too early." Rosa smiled. She knew what was coming.

"Rosa, would you care to accompany me to the Lyceum Theatre in Crewe? You would be able to stay at mine. Separate bedrooms of course. All above board." Rosa didn't know what to say. She kept a smile fixed on her face

"The play is Robinson Crusoe" he added. Splendid, thought Rosa. Robinson Crusoe. Robinson Bloody Crusoe. No man is an island they say. They obviously haven't met George Bradfield.

"That would be lovely" she said, with a control of her considerable temper that was miraculous.

Rosa refused to let the minor misunderstanding of that Sunday get in the way of one of the best Christmases for some years. Whatever his faults, George was a real gentleman and she had been out with some unholy swine in her time. Rosa and George continued to meet up every Sunday, with George typically getting the last train home and climbing into bed some time after 1am. On occasions he would roll into work on Monday looking slightly sleep-deprived. Stickland smiled knowingly. Placing a cup of navy-strength tea in front of George he would whisper a conspiratorial encouragement "You dirty dog." It was, of course, useless to disabuse him.

On the day of the pantomime, Rosa arrived in Crewe just before 4 in the afternoon. George met her at the station and they ate tea at Mrs Minshull's. The two women got on with each other unexpectedly well. Mrs Minshull made sure to show Rosa to her room. It was on the other side of a squeaky landing from George's room. "For obvious reasons" added Mrs Minshull. She also went to some lengths to show Rosa how to lock her door from the inside. "Because we both know what they can be like" she said, and looked at George rather sternly. Rosa smiled and gave George a mock stern look herself.

They walked to the Lyceum wrapped up in their winter coats, arm in arm, hands in pockets. It was a clear night and the stars were visible. Rosa gazed heavenward.

"Do you know the names of any of them?" she asked, gesturing upwards.

"Well that's the constellation of Orion" answered George, pointing in the same direction.

"OK." Rosa thought she knew this already, but humoured him. George pointed out Betelgeuse and Rigel and then turned much further around.

"Over there are the Pleiades, otherwise known as the seven sisters."

"I can only see four of them."

"Look out of the corner of your eye" he suggested.

"Oh yes, there are five, six, seven!" Rosa was enchanted "Do you know any more?"

"Well, if we turn over here" he pointed and they both turned further round "You can see the Big Dipper, part of the Great Bear. That bright star on the right of the arc is Alioth. It's 80-odd light years from us. The light we see today left the star about 1858."

"Good heavens" exclaimed Rosa, and laughed at the unintended pun.

"Now, over here" he waved his hand in a vague zigzag "Can you see a W shape in the sky?"

"Yes I can! What's that?"

"That's Cassiopeia. Named after a queen of unrivalled beauty."

"That's me!" Rosa smiled.

"She was also vain."

"Guilty as charged."

"And finally, this star here." George's arm moved to the left of Cassiopeia, but not as far as the Big Dipper.

"The one that looks all on its own?" asked Rosa.

"Yes. That one is Polaris. The Pole Star. That star never moves from being at true north."

"That's you. Constant and unwavering" smiled Rosa. And all alone, she left un-said.

"You're my Pole Star." she said snuggling up to him "I'm getting cold, shall we go in." They had arrived at the theatre. George held the door for Rosa and they went inside. The foyer was a warm relief from the chilly night. On the walls posters advertised the shows of the New Year, whilst ahead of them a modest, snaking line queued for the confectionary kiosk. There was the same indeterminate smell that theatres and cinemas always have. A melange of upholstery, popcorn, floor wax and brass polish.

"Would you care for some sweets?" asked George.

"They're always frightfully expensive. We should have gone to the newsagent on the way" answered Rosa, rather dejectedly.

"I think we can indulge ourselves, just for one day" and he led them to the back of the queue. As the queue inched slowly forward they had, at last, a full view of the goods on sale. Fry's, Cadbury's and Basset's were conducting their own Great Game, fighting for their sphere of influence over the small glass booth. George and Rosa discussed the merits of each but quickly arrived at the conclusion that chocolate limes suited the pantomime atmosphere.

A gentle tide of people swept them through to the auditorium and they took their seats. Rosa had never been to a Christmas pantomime and so took all the details in. The décor was ostentatious but rather better than a cinema and seemed to allude to a kinder, more gentle age. The audience looked slightly out of place, being mostly composed of harassed parents trying to control their offspring who, in turn, wanted either to run up and down the aisles or to sleep in the coarsely upholstered chairs which offered little comfort unless you sat on them in the prescribed manner.

Once the show began a degree of calm fell upon the audience. The noisy, vibrant cacophony of life now transferred on to the stage. The impresario, a Mr Fortescue, had assembled a cast drawn variously from journeymen entertainers, local schools and the animal life of Gandey's Comedy Circus. Rosa was enchanted and George felt a certain pride at having arranged things so well.

The performance rattled along with great pace and it felt that the triumphant finish came all too early. Rosa was giddy with a girlish delight. "That was the best show I've seen for a very long time" she enthused.

"Better than Spencer Tracey or Clark Gable?" ventured George.

"Almost" she conceded, and wrapped her arm into his. They joined the rest of the erstwhile audience now queuing patiently to exit the theatre. Almost to a man the talk was of the performance. Was their favourite part the Cannibal King? Or the kicking mule? Was it Jimmy's comedy as Billy Crusoe or Kitty's charming Principal Girl? The only agreement was on quite how splendid the evening had been. They exited into the cold night. The air was less clear now, laden heavy with coal smoke from innumerable domestic hearths. The stars were scarcely visible, only one shining through with any vigour.

"Is that Venus?" asked Rosa.

"No, it's too late in the evening. It's Sirius – the dog star" concluded George.

"Oh."

For some reason the stars had ceased to enchant either of them, at least for the moment. They walked back to Mrs Minshull's exchanging small talk, both with their minds on other things. The walk home was nearing its conclusion all too rapidly. George thought of his Father's poetry book. The poem with that line "The unforgiving minute". Kipling probably. His Father had a habit of spicing up a sermon with one of Mr Kipling's slices.

George thought also of the egg timer. Years ago his Mother had dropped their egg timer and it broke about its centre. George, full of youthful curiosity had studied it. The aperture through which the sand flowed was visible in cross section. It seemed impossibly small. Little by little George let the sand escape onto the worktop, until there was none left. Only then was he struck by the finality of it. There was now no way to put the sand back into the glass bulb. He felt faced with a similar dilemma. For, once he spoke, there would be no way back. It was an irreversible process.

Rosa sensed that George was deep in thought, and knowing him as she did left him to it. Presently he would rejoin the human race, and in the meantime she would tell him of the details of her day. They had reached the front gate now. George slipped back into the real world. If he was going to say anything he had scarcely a dozen seconds in which to act. He cleared his throat and manoeuvred himself between the front door and Rosa.

"Rosa Consett, would you do me the honour of being my bride? Of becoming Mrs Rosa Bradfield?" Rosa looked at him as if he had said something quite batty. She had in the past few weeks resigned herself, somewhat unhappily, to a long courtship. In her mind was a profound conviction that she had either misheard him or George was attempting some kind of humour.

"Don't say that. Don't ask that question if you don't mean it. It's just cruel" she answered.

"But I do mean it" said George, rather pleased. It felt right that he had to convince her of his sincerity. She was indeed a prize that had to be fought for, not just plucked from some shelf or meadow.

"George, I'm warning you. It is a beastly thing you are doing by pulling my leg in this way." George was becoming rather more concerned. What further act could convince her of his good faith. The knee of course! He bent down in front of her, one knee resting on the cold damp pavement. He could smell the disinfectant Mrs Minshull used to wash the step with.

"Rosa Sarah Consett, would you do me the honour of being my wife? I couldn't be more sincere. I will love you even as the last star goes out in the heavens." Rosa realised with a thrill he was indeed serious.

"Mr George William Robert Bradfield, of course I will. Now get up from that door step before arthritis sets in." They kissed and embraced. Above their heads there was the noise of a sash window rising. A voice called out:

"Congratulations. And not before time, Mr Bradfield. Now get inside before the pair of you catch your death of cold. I'll put the kettle on" shouted Mrs Minshull. In this manner it was Mrs M who was the first to hear their news.

Mrs Arden finds a Situation.

If hell is other people, thought Philipa, then those guilty of the most heinous sins are sent to the West End at Christmas time. Philipa hadn't been to London since November when she wept her own frozen tears at the cenotaph. It had surprised her. She had been strong and purposeful all her life, not prone to tears or melancholy. However in the past few weeks she seemed to cry at the slightest little thing. When the band played Elgar's Nimrod she just lost control. A kindly soul put an arm around her shoulder and then she got annoyed with herself. It was so long ago, for goodness sake. Move on you silly girl, he wouldn't have wanted any of this. And then she sobbed again, but in anger at all the pomp and majesty with which the nation masked a slaughter. I stand here, not as widow but as witness, to the boys you wasted and will waste again. To the talent you will defile and the beauty you will mutilate. Did they give their lives that I might shop for gilded fancies in Oxford Street?

Now actually in the West End, she took refuge from the yuletide melee in a quiet, overpriced café close to Selfridges. Philipa chose a seat by the window, and peered out at the hapless Christmas shoppers. Few of them looked very happy, and many were wearing a scowl of grim determination. She ordered coffee and a cake and pondered her book. It was nearing completion. There were avenues yet to be explored, maybe by Philipa in later editions, perhaps by others after publication. It was, however, the first draft of the truth, and for this initial edition one of the few remaining decisions was whether or not to preface it with a verse. Philipa had selected "Goosey goosey gander", a subtle reference to Cromwell and his puritan cohorts, but the publisher was not happy and the Statesman was at best ambivalent. Damn them all. It was her book after all, and she wasn't going to airbrush out Cromwell's imperfections. Well, if they insisted she would instead quote the great man himself:

> "I desire you would use all your skill to paint my picture truly like me, and not flatter me at all; but remark all these

roughnesses, pimples, warts and everything as you see me, otherwise I will never pay a farthing for it."

Having settled the matter of the verse, Philipa reviewed her purchases. She had bought all her Christmas presents with the exception of one. It was for a man, of course. They're always the most difficult to buy for. It is hard to navigate between unwarranted familiarity and bland predictability. Not for Philipa the safety of handkerchiefs or socks. The right gift was important, and more so since he had invited her to join him for Christmas. Goosey goosey gander. A spark of inspiration had hit home. She quickly finished her snack, paid the bill and slipped across the road, disappearing into the subterranean world of Bond Street tube station. Minutes later she emerged on Tottenham Court Road and strode confidently into Foyles bookshop. Philipa held the store in no great affection, its Byzantine ways exasperated her on every visit, but she knew it would have exactly what she was looking for. Half an hour later, somewhat weary but with her Christmas shopping complete, she was in a cab heading for Canonbury Square. The traffic was barely moving and she allowed the cab driver to engage her in conversation.

"From out of town, sweetheart?"

"Yes, I'm visiting friends for Christmas."

"Oh lovely. I love Christmas, I do. You should be with those you love." Philipa agreed.

"Bought all your prezzies?"

"I've just finished."

"What's Santa bringing you?"

"Oh, I don't know" Philipa replied coyly, she wasn't really expecting anything. Indeed it dawned on her nobody had really asked what she might want. She tried to remember when she had last been asked. Not for a long time, at any rate.

"Well, what do you want?"

"Oh nothing special. Just peace on earth and goodwill to all men."

"Blimey! You don't want much do you? Well the best of British, that's what I say. A bit of peace and goodwill would go down a treat round here." At this point the traffic made an unexpected surge forward and the driver slammed the cab into gear and shot forward, lest an unscrupulous car might fill the space that had opened up.

Philipa was thrown back into her seat and then forward as he pulled up inches from the car in front. The traffic was stationary again and the cab quiet save for the dull throb of the engine.

"Sorry about that darling. You've got to have your wits about you driving in this town."

"I'm sure" replied Philipa, regretting she hadn't taken the tube.

"So whereabouts on Canonbury Square?" Philipa repeated the address.

"Don't think I know that one. I think that Evelyn Waugh lives round there. Dropped him off once. Hardly spoke a word though. You visiting anybody I'd have heard of?" asked the cabbie bluntly. Philipa paused for a second before replying. She wasn't inclined to give too much away but reasoned there was little harm in telling him.

"The Statesman! Now there's a name from the past. A real gentleman. Not like the current shower. I had him in the cab once. Him and his lovely daughter. Bloody tragedy, pardon my French, him losing his missus and all that. Is he still going strong?" Philipa replied in the affirmative.

"He still with the Liberals?"

"Yes he is."

"I suppose he would be. He's not one of those that blows with the wind. Still, I'm surprised he hasn't retired yet. He'll be fighting the good fight to the end, no doubt. Wonder why he bothers though?"

"I think he wants to make a difference. To make the world a better place, if that doesn't sound too pompous."

"Well good luck to the man, I wouldn't mind living in his Jerusalem. He's got his work cut out at the moment. Can't understand why he bothers. Man like him, deserves a bit of peace and quiet in his old age. Spend some time with that pretty little daughter of his."

"No doubt there's something in what you say" conceded Philipa.

"Too bloody right there is, pardon the lingo again, my darling." Philipa waved her hands as if giving him carte blanche for further profanity.

"I mean..." the cab driver inhaled a deep breath "...it's a grim old world we live in, ain't it? All these bully boys blaming it on the Jews or whoever. I grew up with a load of Jewish lads. Good boys they were. So they don't celebrate Christmas? Can't say I understand it.

Like my old man used to say – what sort of religion doesn't celebrate Christmas? But so what? Live and let live, that's what I say."

"Quite so" agreed Philipa, trying hard to follow this peripatetic monologue.

"Now, some might say we're going nowhere at the moment." Philipa was uncertain whether he was talking about the present journey, the conversation or the wider political context.

"The way I see it though, things ain't all that bad. Our council put up some new houses last year. You should see them! There as good as the villas those stockbrokers live in. Bathroom and indoor loo. They've even got a good sized garden. *Really* beautiful. And they're not too fussy about letting them out to the likes of me. All you have to do is put you name down and pay the rent on time. You and your Statesman mightn't think it's a big thing, but it would mean a lot to me and Pearl."

"Pearl?"

"The lady wife, Chancellor of the Duchy Kilburn." At which he laughed heartily.

"It seems to me that we're not going to have any big step forward until people start behaving better to each other. And we're not going to get people to behave better until we've had our big step forward. So it's one of those viscous circles they're always on about in the papers." At that moment the traffic in front crawled slowly forward. The cab driver was silenced, riding the clutch to allow progress at such a slow pace. They couldn't have been going more than four miles an hour, but they managed to cover the entire length of Rosebery Avenue before coming to a stop.

"No, sweetheart, I can't see anybody being elected on the slogan *We must love one another*". But it's a nice idea. They'll be no great progress in my lifetime, no new dawn. But things just get better all of their own accord, don't they? If you leave people to get on with their lives, that is." His sermon over, the cabbie looked at the buildings around them, seemingly in search of further inspiration, but none was forthcoming and they rode for the rest of the journey exchanging the usual pleasantries about the weather and the season.

On arrival, Philipa tipped the driver a generous amount and wished him and his family a Merry Christmas. Addressing her as "Princess" he wished her the same and implored her to pass his regards on to The Statesman. The housekeeper met her with a flinty stare that suggested she knew all the secrets of Philipa's heart. Philipa was not so easily intimidated and was escorted with greater courtesy into the front room. The housekeeper disappeared to find the gentleman of the house, whilst Philipa took a seat.

It was a fairly soulless room, lacking any personalisation. It was a man's house, despite the ministrations of the housekeeper. It was also clearly a house used only intermittently. The hard, black leather arm chair was cold though there was a roaring fire in the grate. In the distance a conversation was in progress, the housekeeper was by turns annoyed and then concerned. Another voice, commanding an impertinent authority became audible, a voice familiar only for the occasional lilts that interrupted its received pronunciation. The conversation continued even as the participants walked now towards the room Philipa was in.

"Mrs Arden, it's so good to see you again" said a beaming Myfanwy.

"And you too, but please, call me Philipa" she replied, holding out her arms in greeting. Myfanwy embraced her and then stepped back to take her in anew.

"Mary Poppins!"

"Myffy, fy cariad."

"You speak Welsh?"

"Not really, but I did buy a better phrasebook after our last meeting."

"Well you should be careful who you call cariad when you're in the big smoke." she teased, now wearing her Cardiganshire accent with the same pride an undergraduate wears their college scarf.

"Daddy's been called away. Some grave threat to the Empire requiring discussion on privy council terms. Personally I think it was a ruse to meet his chums at the Reform Club."

"Is he back to full health?"

"He's good for six hours a day, though he thinks he can manage ten" Myfanwy laughed indulgently. Philipa smiled.

"Are you any good at decorating a Christmas tree?"

"It's been a while" answered Philipa wistfully.

"Twelve months?"

"More like twenty-odd years."

"Well don't worry. They say it's like riding a bike. You never forget. You'll have to help me bring the tree through." And with that

Myfanwy took Philipa by the hand and led her through to the rear of the house. There stood a Norwegian spruce, so recently separated from the forests and fjords that it dropped scarcely a needle as they wrestled it through the kitchen and into the front room. Back in the front room a flushed Philipa removed her jacket. The housekeeper entered with a bucket full of stones, and between the three of them they stood the tree at an angle close enough to vertical.

"Shall I fetch some tea and cake through whilst we decorate the tree?" suggested the housekeeper.

"That would be lovely, thank you Mrs Vernon."

"No problem my dear. Earl Grey or Darjeeling?"

"Oh, this will be thirsty work. Ceylon. In mugs. With extra milk."

"As you wish" and the housekeeper departed with an all knowing smile to both of them. Myfanwy now led Philipa down into the cellar where they retrieved the decorations which had been hibernating in the damp darkness these last eleven months. Loaded down with sagging cardboard boxes advertising brands that had ceased to exist sometime in the early 'twenties, the two girls then made their way back up the steps. Like a pair of ten year olds they excitedly removed package after package. There were items dating back forty years, valuable only for sentimental reasons. There were exotic objects from the far Empire and gaudy, overpriced baubles that had been bought in a hurry by someone who had more money than they had spare time. Finally there were simple homemade ornaments, created by a skilled hand that had worked by candle light in the dying days of the last century.

"These were my Mothers" explained Myfanwy, holding now a small oval frame containing a sepia picture. Philipa recognised it from the picture magazines of her youth.

"She really was beautiful, wasn't she?" responded Philipa.

"Do you think I look like her?" No false vanity, but genuine interest.

"Oh yes. And she would be so proud of you" answered Philipa, touching the side of Myfanwy's face lightly with her hand. There was a long pause. Philipa smiled awkwardly, concerned she may have been too familiar. But the younger woman smiled back and hugged her, their heads rested on each other's shoulders, bosoms squashed together.

"You know the biggest regret I have in losing my Mum?" reflected Myfanwy, pulling away slightly.

"Tell me."

"It's never having had a brother or sister."

"You would have been welcome to mine!" retorted Philipa, remembering the combination of piety and philandering that made up her siblings.

"You don't mean that?"

"Probably not, but my family are a rum crowd. I would have loved to have a sister like you." And with that Philipa hung the first bauble upon the tree. They continued talking as they worked. Philipa had never been enthusiastic about decorating Christmas trees. There had always been a book to read or another cerebral activity to occupy her. Now, however, she found a degree of serenity in hanging another family's ornaments about this tree. How many people had she decorated a Christmas tree with in her lifetime? It couldn't be more than half a dozen, all of them close relations. It made the current act seem like an initiation ceremony. A welcome into this fragment of a nuclear family.

The Coelacanth

The Statesman sits on the opposition benches with just twenty colleagues. That the party is in decline is self-evident. Less than 7% of the popular vote in the last election. The leader, Mr Samuel, defeated and thereafter replaced by Mr Sinclair. There is a separate group – The National Liberals – who sit on the government benches. They managed to get 33 of their number into the Commons, but they're a reactionary bunch having more in common with the Tories than any principled stand on liberty.

Of the genuine Liberals most hang on through one quirk or other. They're a ragged band of individuals. You would expect no less. They largely represent the Western and Northern fringes of the island. Places where the 19th century faith in personal liberty has yet to be extinguished. Some are returned because of past triumphs, others slip through by skilfully playing the Left off against the Right. A few are returned through sheer hard work. The Statesman for his part has become an advocate for his constituents in a manner that would have attracted derision from his fellow gentlemen in the 1906 parliament. He chairs a weekly surgery, taking in the poor and the huddled masses, hearing their woes and doing all in his power to help. And it is remarkable what can be achieved by a piece of impartial advice, a letter to the right department, a phone call from his office or a quiet word with a minister in the Commons tearoom. He is, in practice, an advocate for the disadvantaged, not a politician. That he makes a difference is acknowledged in all the towns and villages he represents. It is not the exercise of executive power but it is a localised good.

It's now the evening of Friday, 23rd December. Philipa and Myfanwy are taking a childish delight in playing parlour games whilst the Statesman watches on indulgently and tends to his favourite briar. George and Rosa have just stepped off the train at Reading to ask for Rosa's hand in marriage. George leans into Rosa and points out Venus, the evening star, trailing now behind the setting sun. That sun will one day set upon this Empire, but not tonight. Tonight it is racing across the Atlantic, already illuming Bermuda and Newfoundland, soon to shine on the Dominion of Canada before moving on to the possessions in the Pacific and Indian oceans, to the Commonwealth of Australia, The Empire of India and finally tomorrow, to the Union of South Africa.

The evening star has just faded from the South African sky. Hendrik Goosen paid it no heed as he brought his trawler into East London harbour. As is his habit, he calls a friend, Mrs Marjorie Courtenay-Latimer, curator of the small local museum. She has a look through his catch, seeking perhaps a fine specimen to add to the modest museum collection. A blue fin catches her eye. The fish is five foot long, mauve with silver markings. It has a certain primitive beauty to it. On returning to the museum she tries to find it in her reference books, but she cannot. She tries a friend of hers, a Professor Smith, but he is away until after Christmas. Her options for preserving this fish are limited, so it is sent to a taxidermist. When Professor Smith does return he will recognise the fish as a Coelacanth. A fish that biology had previously declared to be extinct 65 million years ago. In the years to come it will be found elsewhere in South Africa, as well as Mozambique and Tanzania. And, before the century is out, a second species from the family Latimeriidae will be found in Indonesia.

The Coelacanth was thought to be extinct. That judgement was based on its disappearance from the fossil record. But the fossil record is a tenuous and treacherous resource, because it never captures more than a fraction of the animals of that species. The Coelacanths did indeed vanish from shallower waters at the end of the Cretaceous period but continued to thrive in the deeper waters of the Indian Ocean. As it is for the Coelacanths, so it goes for the Night Watchman, the Statesman, the Chemist, the Historian, the Engineer and the Shopkeeper.